Finding Spencer

Ruth Gordon

Contents

Chapter 1

Spencer hadn't packed enough layers.

To be fair to herself, she hadn't been thinking clearly when she booked the last-minute flight the previous night. It was, to say the least, a challenge to multitask when she was half-focused on the pending unexpected and expensive transaction and half-focused on trying not to trip over the empty bottle of Merlot she dropped on her dirty, thrifted rug five minutes prior. Never mind the pile of snot-filled tissues thrown haphazardly around her apartment, courtesy of the broken heart she was currently nursing.

Introducing: Spencer, the mess playing dress up as a miracle.

It was hard to focus on, well, anything when it felt like the center of her chest had been gutted and replaced with a fifty-pound weight.

San Francisco International Airport came to her rescue, with refillable water dispensers present almost immediately upon her exit from the plane. While she wasn't nearly as embarrassed about crying her eyes out the entire flight since it wasn't a full bawl session and nobody paid a lick of attention to her, it also meant she was dehydrated by the time she reached her destination. Spencer couldn't refill her water bottle quickly enough, so after downing it with impressive speed, she went for round two.

By the time she slid the bottle into her backpack, she almost forgot how cold it was. (She didn't find airports to be generally cold, unlike how her sister insisted they were.) A cursory glance at the weather app on her phone reminded her that San Francisco was, in fact, not the same climate as Hawai'i. Who knew?

Spencer checked her phone. A new text message alerted her that her guide for the week was on her way. The message arrived about twenty minutes ago, so Spencer replied to let her know her flight had landed.

Since she wasn't sure how long she would need to wait, Spencer thought she would pull herself together as best as possible. Granted, there was a very, very large chance there was no salvaging any part of her appearance that night. Quite frankly, she shouldn't have cared. It was seventy-thirty at night and nobody looked their best at the airport. If someone looked even somewhat presentable, they were kind of an asshole. Who had the nerve to look well-put together at such a soulless place like an airport?

Not Spencer, clearly, if the reflection staring back at her was any indication. Her curls had deflated, her eyes were puffy, and her nose rubbed raw and red. The pimple patch stuck on the side of her chin was less than flattering given the accompanying person to whom it was attached. And that was some kind of... mustard, maybe, stuck on her collar. Spencer couldn't recall accepting the sad excuse of a meal provided by Hawaiian Airlines. Not that it mattered because her hoodie remembered it all too well. She could only imagine how strung out she must have looked to the flight attendant.

"Oh no. I'm so sorry!" A woman appeared next to her carrying a baby who had knocked over her travel-sized bottle of hair oil. "She was so fussy the whole flight."

"All good." Spencer smiled and slid the hair oil back into her clear pouch.

The woman rubbed her hand in circles on the baby's back. "It's freezing here, isn't it?"

Spencer's eyes drifted down to the ALOHA Collection bag. Various baby items stuck out as if reached for in haste during the flight.

"Yeah, a little bit."

Her phone pinged with a new text notification. Spencer tried not to think about how before the last twenty-four hours happened, text messages from that person were few and far between. Life got in the way. People didn't just grow up; they grew apart, even when they didn't want to. It was nobody's fault, except that it was also everyone's fault. Life was inevitable, especially when they lived in separate cities, but it didn't mean they weren't making choices every single day.

"I have to go meet my friend," Spencer muttered. The other person and their child were already gone, so she quietly gathered all of her belongings and made her way outside.

Spencer should have packed a heavier coat, but she had no use for them in Hawai'i. The flimsy excuse of outerwear she sported barely protected against the cold air that swept over her as soon as she walked through the automatic doors, eyes scouring around in search of her friend. She wondered how much a person could change in five years. If the young woman who waved goodbye at the airport in Honolulu would be the same woman waiting for her in San Francisco. Would she still be recognizable? Would they brush past each other in haste, only to turn back around and laugh once they realized what had happened? Or would the differences manifest more internally? Perhaps San Francisco had changed her in ways that Spencer could have never predicted or understood.

Her heart raced in anticipation. Surrounded by strangers, in a city she had never stepped foot in before, it finally hit Spencer how out of her element she was. This wasn't like her. She didn't run away so irrationally to a brand-new city. But it wasn't brand-new, was it? Did she not feel a sense of familiarity just knowing that someone who knew her better than almost anyone else in the world lived there?

"Spencer!"

She stopped. Combat boots squeaked as they spun around. Spencer. Spencer. Only one person said her name so delicately, so comfortingly. Time flew backward. Spencer moved forward. None of what she thought she knew when she stepped off that plane made sense.

When they were younger, Sakura and Spencer couldn't be separated. They were joined at the hips, in the mind, through their souls. Everything made sense because they were together through all the best and worst of times. Life happened, of course, and choices were made. When Sakura left Hawai'i five years ago, they weren't as close as they once were, but she had requested that Spencer be the one to drop her off at the airport. Spencer thought it was strange at first, thinking that Sakura had so many other friends at that point who could have taken her. But then she sat there idling at the airport curb, staring at the empty seat next to her, and realized how much she needed that. That door closed while many other open doors waited for them, even if they existed in different cities.

As they stood there staring at each other from a distance, almost reunited but not quite yet, not until they both moved, Spencer thought back to the day she said goodbye and how the emotions from it still lingered in that foreign air. She had never been more happy to see Sakura. No, not happy. Relieved. Completely and utterly relieved that they were finally back in each other's lives. Not that their presence and impact had ever left. But memories weren't the same as being there in person.

Spencer smiled and waved. After only a few minutes, she decided nothing looked as good as Sakura and San Francisco.

Chapter 2

Saying goodbye to Sakura as she moved away from Hawai'i felt like helplessly watching the door close on the most formative time of her life.

It stung to let go of her childhood, of the life she once dreamed of manifesting in half-empty scrapbooks and long-forgotten Pinterest boards. Saying goodbye forced her to acknowledge that life rarely worked in the ways everyone envisioned for themselves.

She remembered it in shattered flashes of kaleidoscopic light—the bright warmth of summer sun rays hitting her tan skin, sporadic warnings above doors not meant to be entered, the sparkle of a child's eye when they were surprised with the news they would be in Disneyland soon. Spencer couldn't quite recall the exact look on Sakura's face as she waved from the security line, but she remembered how seeing it made her feel. When she returned home, her sister Morgan asked if she was okay because she looked like she had been crying.

"Leave me alone," Spencer had said, rubbing away at her smudged eyeliner.

Getting used to a life without Sakura didn't happen overnight. Truthfully, it started before she stepped on that plane. And it took years for any of it to feel some-what normal. Spencer, Sakura, and Hawai'i. Spencer and Hawai'i. Sakura and San Francisco. Spencer. Sakura. They were two people living in different cities, growing into different lives, who could recognize each other's laughter no matter where they went. Yet Spencer found herself rewatching old videos of their time together, reminiscing about a friendship that lived somewhere in the recent past.

Sakura used to wear her hair in a pixie cut throughout high school, but now, it hung in soft waves that softened the sharp angles of her face. She dressed differently than the last time they saw each other—more polished, more mature—but her face retained a youthfulness that reminded Spencer of all their years spent together.

"Spencer! Hi!"

They embraced. Sakura always had a habit of squeez-ing so tightly that Spencer had a hard time breathing. At that moment, she needed it more than anything.

"How was your flight?" Sakura stepped back. The scent of her favorite tiare-scented oil was unmistakable. "Does the food still suck? Did you get any sleep?"

Spencer swallowed, suddenly overwhelmed again by the reality of what she was doing. But had nowhere to turn back to. No flight she could easily book and hop on at that time at night. And even if she could, she couldn't return to her apartment. Not while he was likely still packing up the last of his things. Spencer couldn't handle going home to the skeleton of her relationship. She wasn't prepared just yet to pick up all the pieces and find new places for them to exist. A new way for her to live her life.

So instead, she smiled at her old friend. It didn't take away the pain from the wound she had spent the last few days nursing, but it did heal the ache left behind since that day at the airport, even if only for a moment.

"It was great. Food still sucked. And no, but I did watch Crazy Rich Asians twice," she rattled off like a grocery list.

Her laugh boasted incredible healing properties, and Spencer tried not to let her head spin thinking about how many storms she could have weathered with it in her life for the past five years.

"Have you even traveled if you didn't watch Crazy Rich Asians?"

"I can hardly remember a flight before 2018."

They stared at each other for a moment, taking the other in. The unspoken truth that they had a lot to catch up on lingered, but airports were lousy places to unload all of their feelings. Sakura pulled away, allowing the years to sit quietly between them, before she took the suitcase handle from Spencer's hand before the latter could insist on pushing her own bag. She didn't want to admit that she had been using it to keep herself standing upright while in transit.

"Did you download the card I told you about?"

Spencer nodded. Double-clicked the right side of her phone. She wasn't sure how much rides cost in the Bay Area, but, based on what little Sakura said so far, that was going to be their main form of transportation for the week. The Clipper card she added to her Apple Wallet was loaded with $20 for now. The attempts made to research how public transit worked in San Francisco were cut short by Spencer's inability to focus on anything that wasn't a rewatch of a movie she had seen more than ten times.

"It's a little bit of a ride to my place. And we gotta transfer. But it'll pass before you realize it, yeah?"

There were no objections on her end. "No problem. Lead the way." Spencer paused before tacking on a quick, "Thank you for—" Deep breath. "Just... thank you."

In her lived experience, women had an uncanny ability to communicate a lot through a simple look—both through the delivery and upon receipt. Reading the room, Sakura smiled at her, gave her another squeeze, and then used her free hand to pull her friend along. They traversed up the escalators, across the short bridge, and the rest of the way to the designated BART platform.

Sakura blew a kiss at the gate. "BART, my beloved. Say hello to Spencer."

She must have been tired because Spencer followed up the silence from the inanimate object with a "Hey, BART."

"Don't let anyone tell you otherwise," Sakura cautioned as she walked through the turnstile. "We love BART."

"Better than that overpriced rail we have back home." Maybe Spencer was bitter about all the construction she endured dodging on her way to work for a rail that went far over budget and went nowhere near where she could use it to get to and from work. Nobody in San Francisco was the wiser. They were blessed with great public transit.

It didn't take long for their ride to arrive. Sakura directed them to a spot near the middle of the car where she could easily hold onto Spencer's suitcase. A handful of other people were scattered around, many hauling on various luggage pieces. The lights induced a minor headache, but once they were on the move, Spencer mostly ignored it. She was too distracted by the people watching and the first glimpses of a new city. Not that there was much to see at that time of night while sitting in the middle of a moving vehicle.

If BART wasn't as loud as it was—the internet warned her the noise sounded like something straight out of the depths of hell at times—Spencer might have put in her earphones. She didn't want to miss anything Sakura might try to point out to her. Unfortunately, she couldn't live out her cinematic dream of pretending to be the protagonist of a cult classic indie film. Instead, she settled for being Spencer and San Francisco sitting alongside Sakura and San Francisco. She supposed that made them Spencer, Sakura, and San Francisco.

Spencer didn't spend much time practicing becoming someone other than Spencer and Hawai'i. She had only traveled outside of her home a handful of times. Most of them were with family. The closest she came to traveling with Sakura was a fifth-grade field trip to the Big Island, but that didn't count. Not in the slightly terrifying way that flying to San Francisco by herself did. Many people traveled solo, but Spencer wasn't one of those people. She almost considered paying to check her bag but was intimidated by the self-service kiosks.

They had six nights. Not a long time in the grand scheme of things. In just a few hours, the first of them would be over already. Spencer didn't want to think too hard about that. She dreaded stepping back on that flight home realizing she spent the entire time staring at the sand slipping through time's fingers. Almost as much as she dreaded the idea of returning home at all.

A few minutes later, Spencer's eyes drifted closed. She didn't consciously notice when she leaned her head against Sakura's shoulder, inhaling that sweet tiare scent once again. But when Sakura shifted her body to make the position more comfortable for them both, Spencer sunk into the feeling.

Chapter 3

Spencer woke to the angelic sound of Sakura singing in the shower. Once upon a time, that was a regular occurrence. They used to joke about how, because Sakura was a morning bird and Spencer a night owl, she didn't need an alarm clock. All she needed to start her day off right was the sound of her best friend's beautiful singing.

She couldn't have asked for a better view. They didn't have a chance to soak any of it in last night since Spencer was so tired by the time they got off the bus, but the Castro District was exactly the kind of place she imagined Sakura living. Thankfully, she wrapped herself in a blanket before stepping out onto the small balcony because the temperature was still far colder than she was used to. Her breath materialized in front of her with each rise and fall of her chest. She closed her eyes and took a few more of them quietly, allowing herself to wake up gradually with the rest of the city.

Six thirty. It was a miracle to be up that early, but she probably had the peaceful sleep from last night to thank for that. She didn't get nearly enough of it on a day-to-day basis. Work stressed her out. Family stressed her out. Her boyfriend stressed her out. Ex-boyfriend. She still had to get used to calling him that. Even though their relationship deteriorated a long time ago and had been on a slow, painful march down the road to extinction for the past year, she still counted on that label to help keep her afloat. If they were still in a relationship, they didn't have to admit defeat. They didn't have to accept they failed at tending to a relationship they once believed in. However, it didn't do much good because she spent most nights tossing and turning, desperate to stay lost in her dreams but cursed to find herself waking up right at all of the good parts.

The balcony door slid open and Sakura stepped out with a towel wrapped around her head. She took the other free chair situated amongst the potted plants and outdoor trinkets, including a ceramic toad wearing a top hat.

"Sleep alright?" she asked.

Spencer accepted the mug of jasmine tea. Some things never changed, including Sakura's morning rituals of shower and hot tea.

"You didn't need to sleep on the couch. I'm the one who sprung a surprise visit on you so last minute."

The two of them had been watching movies in Sakura's room, and then suddenly, Spencer was waking up the next morning. She didn't recall them having much of a conversation once they reached the apartment, nor did she remember a blanket being tucked around her. Thankfully, Sakura used silk pillowcases. Her hair didn't look as electrified as it did most mornings when she forgot to protect it.

"That's funny you thought I would let you sleep on the couch," Sakura scolded. She waited a few moments to let Spencer take a sip of her tea. "So, is it ridiculous of me to think you might have looked up things to do while you were here or—"

Spencer laughed. "Funny you thought I used more than a single brain cell when I booked my ticket."

"Well, you made it here so I think I would consider that an impressive output for one brain cell."

"Have you always been here? In Castro?"

Sakura shook her head. "Moved about a year and a half ago. I spent so much time coming here that it just made sense."

"And how are you liking it?"

"Best place in the whole world. Well, except for home."

"It feels very... you."

On one hand, Spencer wasn't sure if she was qualified to make that assessment anymore. On the other hand, as evidenced by the rest of the morning so far, some things truly never changed.

Sakura never had a problem being herself. Or if she did, she never let the rest of the world see it. She had a coming out moment, but she prefaced it by saying, in the most eloquent way, this is more of a formality. We all know I'm bisexual as hell. People accepted her without question, which was fortunate since that wasn't the case for everybody's experience. Spencer wondered for a long time if it was so easy for the people who loved her to do so because Sakura accepted herself in a way that left no room for anything else. What she wanted from the world, she put out into it. Or maybe that was a silly lens through which to view her coming out. Either, Spencer admired her for it. Especially when she went through a phase of testing out other labels to see what fit—bisexual, pansexual, omnisexual, oh but maybe pansexual, and then bisexual again. No matter how many detours and stops she took along the way, Sakura seemed to appreciate the journey of figuring herself out. Always one to enjoy the ride.

Off in the distance, Spencer caught a glimpse of the rainbow crosswalks. Almost every other house had some kind of pride flag hanging up. The district screamed of its pride and acceptance and love for one another, which made it so easy to feel comfortable waking up in it when Spencer was still trying to wrap her head around waking up in this new city for the first time. Day one and Spencer already felt revitalized.

"What time do you normally head to work?" Spencer asked.

Sakura had given her the spare key last night, so she figured she would have to spend most of her time exploring the city by herself, but Spencer wasn't sure about her exact work schedule. It appeared to be pretty easy to get around, so that worked in her favor. Google Maps would be her best friend. San Francisco seemed like the kind of place where one could keep walking without a specific destination in mind and eventually stumble upon something unique and interesting.

"I have to leave in thirty but it's just for today. I took the rest of the week off so I can show you around."

It was probably a little silly to play coy since she had already imposed the trip on her, but Spencer scrunched her nose. "The whole week? You didn't have to, oh my g—"

Sakura stripped the towel from her head and shook her hair out in such a smooth, hypnotic motion that Spencer looked away for no other reason than she thought she should.

"First time we've seen each other in five years and you think I'm not gonna drop everything for you? Spence, where has your head been?"

They didn't need to exchange any looks to confirm that perhaps that wasn't the best thing to say. Not that it was wrong. But there were a million other versions of that reply that would rank higher in comfort level since they had yet to unpack all of the reasons why they hadn't seen each other and spoken much at all over the last five years. They went from being best friends to occasionally liking each other's stories once in a blue moon. And none of that took into consideration how Spencer clearly didn't have her head on straight be-cause she couldn't even stand to remain on the same island as her ex-boyfriend while she waited for him to pack his things and leave.

"There's a coffee place that's easy to get to that I really like. SPRO. I'll send you the address. They have cool lattes and stuff. Sandwiches are hit or miss, but there's plenty of stuff around here." Sakura rose to her feet. "I'll see if I can cut out early. Call you when I do? Wherever you're at, I can meet you."

Spencer nodded and made a mental note to share her location to make finding each other easier. No plan, just vibes became the new mantra of her trip. She thanked Sakura for the tea, promised that she would lock everything up before when she finally got dressed and left, and returned to her morning view of Castro.

Chapter 4

"That's that Spence espresso."

Spencer blinked.

"Too much?" asked the barista with a wince.

"All good. Thank you."

She dropped a couple of bills into the tip jar before taking her drink over to one of the tables. The thin red chairs that looked like she could snap them in half with her bare hands left a lot to be desired. Thanks to the leisurely pace at which she got dressed, she missed most of the morning rush and found a seat with minimal effort. While she stepped out onto the streets of San Francisco with an open mind, she resembled a baby learning how to walk for the first time. If someone attempted to strike up a conversation with her, Spencer couldn't be sure she had the emotional bandwidth to keep it going. Unfortunately, she also had to steal one of

Sakura's coats because none of the jackets she brought helped. Spencer was glad nobody caught her taking four steps outside of Sakura's apartment building and then immediately going back inside to switch out her outerwear.

While the custard-filled chocolate croissant tasted delightful and the espresso-with-a-tune filled her with the necessary amount of caffeine needed to operate like a functioning adult, Spencer's mind continued to race like an F1 car down the streets of Monaco, only narrowly missing the barriers keeping her in line.

Seven years was a long time for any relationship, but especially one that started her sophomore year of high school. They had known each other for years beforehand, so it made the severance feel even worse. Spencer didn't just say goodbye to the only relationship she had ever been in. She said goodbye to someone she knew from childhood. Someone who had seen her grow up in all of the most embarrassing and honest ways. Even if they were better friends than lovers at different crossroads of their lives, that still meant letting go of something meaningful.

She didn't understand it. Did everyone go through something as devastating as this, multiple times in their life? Obviously, she thought naively. Spencer's heart breaking wasn't some anomaly of the universe but practically a rite of passage. But how did everyone else do it? How did people survive feeling like they had lost a limb? Or like they had actively watched those lost years of their life go up in flames while they stood by helplessly, unable to stop it from burning to ash.

The worst part was that even though the relationship had ended, it wasn't over. When she flew back home and walked into the half-empty apartment, it would puncture her once again. Her finger would hover over delete for every picture they shared on social media, but she inevitably archived the images instead. Any time someone asked her about it, she would have to recall all of the heartbreak in vague details while they stared back at her in the most pitiful way. And whenever she thought about those seven years of her life, she had to relive all of it. The good, the bad, the parts that she wanted to forget, and the parts that she knew she had to hold onto.

Her phone started ringing. Morgan. Spencer took a deep breath and sighed. Rolled her shoulders like she was winding up.

"Hello?"

"Hello? Hello? Spence, where the hell are you? Mom said you're in San Francisco, but I told her that's impossible because why the fuck would you be in San Francisco without telling me?"

If Spencer had taken care of herself instead of hitting snooze on her responsibilities, she wouldn't have ignored the reminder she set six months ago about needing to update her Hawaiian Miles account email to her personal email address instead of her mom's. She never got around to changing it from when her mother created the account for her when Spencer was younger.

"I needed a change of scenery," Spencer said.

Her sister scoffed. "Change of scenery. Right. So you decided to hop on a plane and fly across the Pacific. Casual."

"Did you need something? My coffee's getting cold."

"Are you—what's going on? Seriously."

Spencer and Morgan were close, like many other tight-knit sisters who relied on each other growing up. They told each other everything. So she knew that keeping something like this from her sister would sting once she found out. And as much as she wanted to push the problem onto her future self, Morgan wouldn't stop calling until she figured out what was going on. She knew Spencer didn't up and leave out of the blue like she had. Pretending she could keep the secret any longer would only prove to bite her harder in the ass than owning up to it now.

"We broke up."

If she had to say his name, her breakfast would be all over the table. Thankfully, Morgan didn't need further explanation, nor did she call her out for avoiding the mention.

"When? What happened? Where is he?"

Spencer sighed. Everything rolled in like the morning fog above the bay. She dreamt of the clear blue sky back home that she had woken up to three days ago. Her answer applied to all of the above. "Does it matter?"

"Of course, it matters. That's why you're in San Fran?"

"They hate when you call it that."

"Who? Who's they?"

"San Francisco."

"How can a city hate it when I call it San Fran?"

"People. The people from San Francisco hate when you call in San Fran."

Morgan huffed. "And I'm supposed to care because—"

"You know, you've asked me more questions than not," Spencer pointed out.

"Can you—I don't think you can blame me for that since you didn't even tell me you were leaving the city."

"I left the entire island."

"Even worse. Wait, are you with Sakura?"

They only knew one person who moved to San Francisco. "Yeah."

"Huh."

"What do you mean, huh?"

"Nothing," Morgan answered. "It's just been a while since you talked to her."

A good sister might have spared her the drawn-out back and forth, but, as proven by her sneaking out of Hawai'i, Spencer wasn't being a good sister. And maybe that was okay for now. Maybe she deserved to be selfish and enjoy some time away from everyone. Morgan's heart was in the right place, but it didn't make it any less annoying for Spencer to field questions about her failed relationship.

"Are you okay?" Morgan's voice faded like she quickly pulled away from the phone for a beat. "Just... just tell me you're okay."

"I'm okay." Maybe it wasn't the whole truth, but it was at least some of it. Spencer was sitting at a cute cafe with delicious coffee in San Francisco, courtesy of that broken heart, a savings account that had been mild-ly depleted, and PTO hours banked over years of not taking other vacations. Many would consider her in the middle of a dream spontaneous getaway. "I'll be back on Saturday. Can you pick me up from the airport?"

Her sister laughed, despite sounding frustrated enough not to want to. "Was that your plan all along or—"

"No more questions, please."

"Fine. You're annoying. And weird."

"And I love you."

"Love you too," Morgan said. "Get me a keychain? We're having a long talk when you get back."

"Postcards are so much better."

"Or some pressed pennies. I'll take pressed pennies."

Spencer finished off her espresso. "All three sounds good. See you on Saturday."

Chapter 5

After her quick stop for breakfast, Spencer spent most of the day wandering. She didn't have any-where particular in mind, despite recalling a few interest points off the top of her head. As a novice when it came to traveling, the illusion of choice tormented her. She knew the internet could provide an endless list of places to visit but would have gotten overwhelmed, so she chose the path more leisurely traveled.

Japantown welcomed her with open arms, courtesy of a cozy late-morning stroll through shops that car-ried cute accessories and knick-knacks. She bought too many pens she didn't need, a few blind boxes, which were her weakness, and a couple of manga books that were certainly going to weigh down her carry-on item. While she was tempted to grab lunch there as well, she decided to purchase a bento instead and take a ride over to the Painted Ladies for a picnic. Plenty of people set up along the tall hill straight across from the houses. Spencer thought it charming the way most people didn't seem that occupied with the view in front of them. They enjoyed relishing in nostalgia.

Eventually, she drifted back into the Castro. Stumbled around a few more shops, bought souvenirs for people who may or may not even know she was in San Francisco, and walked with her head down to admire the Rainbow Honor Walk. An old gay couple helped her take pictures with the bronze plaque for Freddie Mercury before they walked away while singing I Want To Break Free.

Spencer walked into a bookstore with a bright purple exterior for a reprieve from the cold. It felt nice to be able to remove her hands from her pockets. Wiggled them around for good measure. Fabulosa Books, the sign above the door read. The front display was simply labeled as Queer Stuff, with a colorful selection of titles handpicked by the staff and written by a diverse collection of authors. Spencer loved reading and couldn't figure out what to check first.

"Welcome to Fabulosa," said one of the employees. They smiled at each other. "Looking for anything in particular today?"

Spencer shook her head. "Just browsing."

"Alright. Let me know if you need any help. 'Kay, babe?"

"Thanks."

In true Spencer fashion, when faced with the torture of endless choice, she scurried over to the small section of the store with stickers, pins, and other small items. She didn't believe in heaven, but if she had, it probably would have looked something like that.

Stickers were her vice. Water bottles, notebooks, her laptop. All of them were covered with stickers, and most were either ordered online from small shop owners or gifted by her sister. While many held the debilitating sticker anxiety that led them to keep their stickers in drawers and folders to collect dust, Spencer had no such problems. She took too much pride in finding places for new stickers, even if that meant retiring an old one.

Better Out Than In read one of the stickers. Shrek's outhouse with a rainbow bursting out. Nice. Spencer giggled under her breath. Only paying two bucks for it felt like a crime, but she was okay with taking advantage of it.

A long row of different pride flags stretched across the upper part of the display table. Spencer always found the Trans and Pansexual flags to be the prettiest colors. The Progress Pride flag never went unnoticed. Her eyes fell onto the Bisexual flag. While Sakura probably owned a billion of these, she snatched up one anyway, just in case she wanted another.

Spencer reached for another bisexual flag again. Let her fingers glide across the smooth surface. She took a deep breath, shook her head, and placed it back onto the pile.

The indie bookstore was well stocked, even considering the small square footage. Not quite at the chaotic level that came off as stuffy and overwhelming. But enough that Spencer knew she could spend hours wandering in front of those shelves. And even then, she would leave knowing that there were plenty of titles she hadn't considered because she didn't have the time. They included extensive sections for different genres, cultures, and identities. Books highlighting Trans lives, Black voices, and Indigenous experiences, whether it be about Pacific Islanders, Native Americans, Palestinians, Africans, or anyone else in between. While she did feel weighed down by the options for her to take home, she had to be cutthroat about her selection. The last thing she needed was to have to pay to check her bag because she bought more than she had room for, especially since she hadn't even stopped by Trader Joe's yet for very necessary snacks to bring home.

"There you are."

Sakura found her flipping through the box of vintage postcards priced at fifty cents each. Spencer already held eight in her hand.

"How'd you find me?" Spencer checked the cat-shaped clock on the wall. A child walking around earlier told her they named it Barbara. According to Barbara, it just turned four o'clock. "Does ditching work early get you into the running for employee of the month?"

"Obviously. They're prepping my portrait as we speak." Even a ruffled Sakura, who endured two-thirds of a workday, stood out in the small gathering of patrons. Pretty enough that people stepping aside for her had no choice but to take a second look. "And I stalked you."

The customer standing next to them looked mildly alarmed. A little older than the average person who utilized their location-sharing capabilities.

"How was work?"

"First rule of being employed—" Sakura pulled her hair up into a ponytail. "—Never talk about work unless you're being paid to."

"Is this your way of saying you don't want to talk about work or that you want me to pay you to answer the questions?"

"I'm fine with either."

Sakura winked. Spencer looked down at her items.

"Let me just pay for these and we can head out."

"I'll be right here." Sakura wandered over to a shelf carrying books about popular queer icons.

Spencer walked over to the register where the employee who first welcomed her stood.

"Ready?" they asked.

She nodded and placed her selections on the table—too many stickers, even more postcards, Beyond the Gender Binary by Alok Vaid-Menon, Gumbo YA YA by Aurielle Marie, and a few pins.

"Nice haul," the cashier said. They tapped the cover of Beyond the Gender Binary. "Love this one. They have such an empathetic view of the world."

"Nice store. Could've emptied my entire wallet in here." Spencer laughed. "And yeah, I've seen some of their interviews. They're great. I'm excited to read this."

"Consider this a thank you for supporting us." They tossed a sticker on top of her pile—a Fabulosa Books sticker.

"Oh, thank you so much." Spencer smiled at them and tapped her card against the reader before seeing a sign on the opposite side of the register. "What's this?"

BOOKS NOT BANS, it read.

"An initiative sponsored by Fabulosa to send LGBTQIA+ books to organizations in conservative parts of the States where access and resources are being heavily restricted to those who need them most," they answered, sliding the sign over so Spencer could take a better look. "We reach out to organizations to see if they would like a box of books. If they do, they tell us what their audience needs so we can select books that serve them the best."

Spencer opened her wallet back up. "Do we buy specific books or—"

"That, or we can accept contributions." They pulled a list of books that were used most often for the boxes. Spencer quickly grabbed a stack of them from around the front of the shop, focusing on Trans, Lesbian, and Black authors. When she returned to the register, they rang them up with a smile. "This is incredibly generous. Thank you, darlin'."

"Thank you for the work you do," Spencer replied. Best $120 she spent in a long time.

After placing the books in the donation box and handing over her purchases with both receipts, the employee placed a business card and a small flyer into Spencer's hands. "Not sure if you're from around here, but we do events sometimes. Drag readings of banned books, live music, raffles, those sorts of things. We also appreciate volunteers who can help with preparing the boxes."

"Oh, I'm not from here. Hawai'i. Unfortunately. I mean, not unfortunately. But... you know what I mean."

They laughed. "No worries. Praying for a free Hawai'i in the very near future."

"Thank you." Spencer pointed at Sakura. "My friend lives here, though. I'll let her know. I'm sure she'd love to help."

"Ah, friend. Yes. Here, take another for her." They handed Spencer another Fabulosa Books sticker. "Enjoy the rest of your time in San Francisco."

Chapter 6

A trip to San Francisco for the first time without stopping to see the famed Golden Gate Bridge amounted to one of the greatest sins, and Spencer couldn't have that on her conscience. International Orange looked good against the background overcast skies. She had enough sunny days waiting for her on her most beloved island. Right then, she relished existing in the cold, observing the fog roll over the bay. Fellow tourists strolled around in their heavy coats, tightly wrapped scarves, and visible puffs of smoke-like air as they breathed in and out. In her head, she heard that familiar voice saying Good Morning, San Francisco. Looks like it's gonna be another awesome day in the Golden City. And indeed, it did. Nothing beat saying good morning with a perfect view of the beauty of the bay.

They hopped off the bus, wadded through the sea of tourists, and found a spot a little further down with fewer people to battle for a great shot. Sakura had navigated them with the expertise of someone who had lived there long enough to not need a map to get around anymore. On the other hand, Spencer worried too much about whether it was painfully obvious that she was a tourist.

Then again, that didn't matter. Popular tourist spots earned that title for a reason, more often than not. She thought about all Hawai'i's "must-see" spots and how she had zero desire to visit them herself, as someone born and raised on the islands. But that didn't mean others weren't allowed to be excited about them.

"Get a good one?" Sakura asked after Spencer snapped a few shots on her phone.

She leaned in close, using her hand to block any glare. Close enough that her hair tickled the side of Spencer's cheeks.

Spencer cleared her throat and pulled away. "Yeah, these look great." She shoved her phone back into her purse and her hands into the pockets of Sakura's coat. "Should we head to that palace you were telling me about? You said it's not that far from here, right?"

Sun filtered through the wispy clouds to illuminate Sakura's smile in a way that inspired the most romantic at heart to pen stories. Spencer looked away, suddenly enamored with the bridge she spent ten minutes taking pictures of.

"You don't want any pics of yourself?" she asked. "We came all this way."

Spencer shook her head. "Oh, no. No. That's okay. These are good."

"Why not?"

"I don't take pictures of myself."

Sakura scoffed. "And I repeat—why not?"

About six months after Sakura moved, Spencer ventured through town and into Waikiki Beach. The last time she went there, and probably only the third in her entire life. She steered clear of Waikiki for most of her life, akin to Las Vegas locals avoiding the strip, but convinced herself that Kanaka shouldn't look down upon any part of their home because of the effects of tourism. She felt like that fed into the colonization and gentrification of her home. Hawaiians, first and foremost, should be able to enjoy any Hawaiian lands.

She wanted to take a picture with the Duke Kahanamoku statue. Beautiful lei hung from each arm, salt air clung to her skin, and the sun had come out to play. They were also celebrating their anniversary with a dinner at one of the fancy hotels she had never seen the inside of in her life, followed by a staycation with plans to lounge by the pool in the morning. By all accounts, a perfect day in the making.

"Here—" Spencer handed her phone over. "Before that giant ass group comes over here."

He hesitated before taking it from her, eyes darting back and forth on either side of them. After a few seconds, he huffed and held it up. She didn't get a warning or even a countdown. He just started taking pictures, most of which she was sure had captured her eyes closed. Because life had incredible comedic timing, a gust of wind picked up just in time to blow her hair directly into her face as well. As soon as the group of strangers had traveled close enough, he shoved it back in her direction, almost dropping the phone in the sane. Spencer barely had any time to check the photos before realizing he had already started walking back toward the hotel for check-in.

Spencer opened her mouth to speak. Then closed it again, tired.

"When did you stop straightening your hair?"

"Huh?" she asked.

He stared at her hair, not in her eyes. Her hair. "You used to straighten it every day, right? It looked pretty like that."

Spencer fingered the ends of her hair. It used to be curlier but after years of heat styling—pressure forced on her by Western beauty standards by which she did not naturally fit—the pattern had loosened up quite a bit. The front pieces still curled up nicely, especially around her fringe, but the bottom layers had deflated into sad waves. (Not that waves were a bad texture.) (And not that people who looked like her didn't receive judgment even with only waves.) A few weeks ago, she decided to embrace her hair in its natural state. Gave herself a personal goal to not touch her straightener for at least the rest of the year. It would take a long time to grow out the damaged part of her hair and adapt a routine to take care of the new growth, but Spencer was determined to make it happen. She didn't want to spend the rest of her life modifying every element of her appearance to fit some standard that, at the end of the day, would never embrace her for herself. The change in her appearance went by mostly without fanfare. On one hand, she didn't want to be ogled like a circus act. On the other, it felt bad to think nobody cared enough to notice the effort she was making.

"I wanted to try something new," she nearly whispered.

He nodded and didn't say anything else.

When Spencer returned home the following night and finally looked over the pictures properly, she confirmed that none of them were decent. Eyes half-closed, endless sun glares, and hair in her face. That small, nagging voice in her head that told her she would never be seen as pretty or beautiful or anything else she wanted to be called by someone she loved, screamed about how ugly and frizzy and dirty her hair looked.

Quietly, she deleted every single picture.

"Come on," Sakura insisted with a persuasive smile. "You'll look great. I promise."

Spencer didn't have it in her to say no, so she handed over her purse and stood at a spot with the best angle of the bridge behind her. Sakura waited for a family to pass before holding up the phone, blocking that perfect, polished smile from view. She started counting down but then stopped and skipped back over to where Spencer stood. The latter waited frozen, wondering if maybe she had taken the picture of all, as she was used to. Instead, Sakura brushed Spencer's waves out of her face and tucked the strands behind her ear.

"When did you start wearing your hair like this again?"

"Um... a few years. Off and on. It's kind of frizzy right now, sorry."

"Frizzy is nice," Sakura replied gently but quickly. She dropped her hand after lingering for a few seconds. "So pretty. It's my favorite when it's like this."

Spencer nodded. Looked down at her feet until Sakura's Converse faded out of frame.

"Thank you," she whispered.

Later that night, back in Sakura's apartment with Japanese Breakfast playing softly in the background, Spencer flicked through all of those moments captured by one of her oldest friends. It might have been that only someone who understood her the way Sakura did could do so in such an honest way. Maybe it was that small part of Spencer's inner self that needed to heal from years of being told how the world could only view her. Perhaps it was a combination of both.

Either way, she didn't delete any of those pictures.

Chapter 7

"**S**o, how are you liking it so far?"

"If it weren't for how I almost passed out walking up that hill yesterday, I would say I could live here."

She couldn't definitively decide if she had fallen in love with the city just yet—was there such a thing as saying she loved something or someone too early? Probably—but she imagined it was the closest she would ever get. Nowhere would ever feel quite like home, but perhaps it was possible to discover a home away from home. A place she wasn't born in, hadn't been raised in, didn't know for much more than 48 hours, and yet found it as familiar and comfortable as if she had. She decided this after only a third morning of waking up by the bay.

Before Spencer arrived in San Francisco, she told herself she wouldn't leave until she accomplished the quintessential San Francisco experience of riding a cable car. But then she arrived, realized how expensive they were, and decided she could continue to dream. After wandering around the streets of Chinatown, they settled on the next best thing—the free cable car museum. It was within walking distance, Sakura had said. But nothing of the hills required to get to the damn thing. Spencer had to stop at multiple points to catch her breath. She even debated paying for a ride up the hill, but that cost as much as the cable car ride would have.

Ultimately, it was worth it, even if she thought she would throw up all those egg tarts she shoved into her mouth minutes before they started walking.

Sakura laughed as she leaned over to grab a small plate of bok choy. The conveyor belt of food continued spinning around with tiny plates overflowing with vegetables. All-you-can-eat hot pot restaurants were guilt-free zones of pure freedom and the perfect way for them to start their Wednesday. (Late, of course.) The only thing it cost her, besides the transit fare, was being mocked by the bus driver for mispronouncing Daly City like daa-lee. Spencer elected not to ask him how he mispronounced Hawai'i and mock him for it.

"You get used to it," she said. "When I first got here, I was so embarrassed by how out of shape I was. I couldn't even escape all the hills at school. Berkeley gave me three very important gifts: a degree, student loan debt, and a pep in my step. Now I walk all the time."

"Oh?" Spencer laughed.

"Well, I kind of have to. No way I'd keep a car in the city. And you've seen these hills. Parking on them still terrifies me."

They paused while the server dropped off their drinks and two plates of meat—pork belly and wagyu.

Sakura dipped a piece of napa cabbage into her sauce. "I went on a hike last week. Voluntarily. Consider me a changed woman."

"I can't remember the last time I hiked," Spencer admitted. "Actually, I do. It was that time I—"

"Wait—I know what you're gonna say..."

"Koko Head," they said in unison.

"I sprained my fucking ankle." Spencer groaned, recalling the unfortunate incident when they were high school juniors. "Worst day of my life."

The most embarrassing part of that day wasn't the sprained ankle. Earlier, the three of them—Sakura, Spencer, and Spencer's boyfriend—stopped to hang out at the playground near their old elementary school. They weren't in the way since it was a Saturday, which was ideal for many reasons but mostly because she didn't make a fool of herself in front of a bunch of kids. Spencer had tried sliding down a part of the playground not designed for said activity, and her foot got caught, sending her face-first into the rubber flooring. After a quick investigation which concluded that she did not lose any teeth in the accident, though she lacked a concerning amount of dignity, the three of them dissolved into balls of laughter and tears.

The part of the day where they went for a hike and procured a sprained ankle thanks to the pain and clumsiness on Spencer's part was less than humorous. Everything else that happened that day made reminiscing on it much more bearable.

"I miss it there," Sakura muttered under her breath, a barely-there smile peeking through the fog of nostalgia. If Spencer hadn't been hanging on to every word between them in their short time together, she might have missed it.

"Can I ask you a question?" Spencer asked.

Sakura nodded.

"Probably just my very limited anecdotal evidence, but I always thought that people who went away for school moved on after they graduated. Like, if I went to Seattle for college, I'd find a job somewhere else after. Seattle would only be the city where I went to school, and I'd find another city to become myself in."

It didn't elude Spencer how naive and out-of-touch she sounded. (A rude categorization, on second thought.) She didn't go to college for two main reasons: she couldn't afford it and she had no idea what she would have studied. Most of what she understood about the college experience was derived from seeing the world around her, whether through people she knew or in the media.

"It can be, for a lot of people," said Sakura. "I guess it depends on where you go to school, what field you're entering. Whether... there are other factors tying you to another place. Or, hell, you end up getting a job that has nothing to do with your degree—" She pointed at herself. "—because the world works in fucking ridiculous ways."

"Why did you end up staying here?" Spencer asked. The question sounded like her friend had settled for something less, but she didn't mean for it to come out like that. Anyone would be lucky to call San Francisco home. Sakura looked away, at the conveyor belt. "We didn't talk as much before you left, but I always thought you'd come back home. I know so many people from Hawai'i leave and don't come back and it's sad, but it's usually because they don't have a choice. You never really... struck me as one of those people."

She regretted bringing it up as a dense silence fell on top of them, not at all with like the comfort of a weighted blanket. Sakura was quiet for so long that Spencer wondered if she could get away with pretending as if she hadn't said anything. They could stare awkwardly at each other, and clear their throats. Sakura would ask her to repeat her question, and Spencer would ask something completely different.

Instead, Sakura let her pot of sukiyaki soup base continue to rise to a rolling boil while their vegetable selections and cuts of meat sat untouched on the table. She fidgeted with already straight chopsticks. Brushed a few strands of hair behind her ear. Finally looked up at Spencer with something behind her eyes that the latter couldn't quite read.

"Well, that was the plan. I couldn't see myself living out of Hawai'i. Not for a very long time. School was meant to be a detour from my life. I did it because it was expected of me—lame, I know. My parents wouldn't have let me not go to college. But I knew it wouldn't define what I did after I graduated. Which, yes, is an extremely privileged thing to say. Just like it's privileged to have gone in the first place." She rambled, occasionally stumbling over her words. "The time came for me to graduate. My parents flew up to visit for the first time since I moved out here and asked me what my plans were after. It made me realize for the first time that, even though they expected me to go to school, they didn't have any plans for me after I was done. All they wanted was to see me get that piece of paper. No more expectations. No more wondering if I had to figure out how to accomplish everything they ever wanted for me. I had the whole world ahead of me. So, I decided not to leave. I had already fallen in love with San Francisco years before. Now I get to fall in love with it more and more every day since."

Spencer opened her mouth to speak.

"But I miss it," Sakura continued. "I miss Hawai'i every day that I'm not with her. I miss the people, I miss who I was, and who I thought I would become. I sometimes wonder what it would be like if I didn't leave. If I didn't... run from a life I didn't think would wait for me. But I'm here, and everything is... good. I'm trying to make the best of what's here. I think I'm doing alright."

Spencer smiled and nodded. "Good. Good for you."

Chapter 8

Unfortunately, Spencer didn't get the opportunity to see Broadway productions often. She couldn't afford to fly out to New York, and any time there happened to be a tour that stopped in Hawai'i, she couldn't find the time to make it out to one of the shows. So, she spent most of her days enviously consuming grainy YouTube videos or available film adaptations that, as beautiful as they were, are never quite the same. She danced around her living room, imagining an alternate life where she might have had the chops to become a musical theatre performer. She didn't have the rhythm, the voice, or overall talent to try.

San Francisco hosted a Wicked production, but her spontaneous budget didn't account for last-minute tickets. Even the very last row of the entire theater was a little more money than she would have expected. Not that she was complaining; she understood the logistics.

Sakura surprised her when she revealed that the Orpheum Theater was next to the farmers market they wanted to check out. If they couldn't see a show together, at least walking by the theater and snapping a few pics of the marquee would be fun.

Sakura and Spencer sat huddled together on the bus to share earphones while listening to the Wicked soundtrack. Listening to two different versions of Defying Gravity, first thing in the morning did more to wake her up than any shot of espresso.

Upon exiting the BART station, the classical opulence of the Orpheum Theater loomed over them like a jewel in the sky. Seeing the iconic Wicked poster high in the air made her smile. One day, hopefully soon, she would get the chance to see it. For now, she settled on taking as many pictures as possible from every single angle. Something that felt more like a formality than anything since she knew most of the images would end up collecting metaphorical dust on a hard drive somewhere in her apartment for years to come. But, quite frankly, she didn't care. Humans sucked sometimes, but the way they all memorialized the best times of their lives made her heart flutter, and reminded her of those quiet, lonely days spent dancing in her living room.

Spencer allowed Sakura to take as many pictures of her in front of the theater as her heart desired. Some on her phone, some on the other. Sakura hyped her up like she was a supermodel, and admired each photo as if they were destined to end up on the cover of Vogue. Upon giving her approval, Spencer recognized the genuine light behind that smile.

As they winded down on their photo session, a couple of girls walked past. Hope danced through the life behind their eyes before being quietly snuffed out. Though they had walked by the theater for a purpose, they also appeared somewhat disappointed by something. A missing puzzle piece in an otherwise perfectly crafted day. If Spencer had to make an educated guess, it probably had something to do with the theater being closed off to the public, and the security guard standing watch in front of the rolling metal door. Like Sakura and Spencer moments ago, the two women started taking pictures with a disposable camera that Spencer hadn't seen someone use in forever.

"Do you want one of the two of you?" Sakura asked, her voice raised so they could hear her over the busy sounds of San Francisco.

"Oh! Yeah, that'd be great. Thank you!" The woman using the disposable camera tucked it into her fanny pack while the other handed off her phone with the camera pulled up.

Spencer couldn't help but notice how well they complimented each other visually. One with long, dark brown hair, and the other with a blonde pixie cut. Combat boots and Converse sneakers. Matching friendship bracelets worn on opposite arms. (Sakura smiled at the sight of their pink, purple, and blue 'bi bi baby' bracelets.) The taller one with the boots wore a black, white, and orange plaid dress with a black sweater that looked big enough to double as a blanket, while the other wore black leggings and a graphic tee of The Mummy characters in a similar color scheme.

"Love the matching," Sakura commented as she handed back the phone with about twenty nearly identical pictures. "The cast of The Mummy was my bi-awakening. Incredible."

"Same," they said in unison, laughing.

"We were hoping the gift shop would be open. Wishful thinking," said the blonde one. She ran her fingers through her hair before tossing a wistful glance back at the theater. A cool morning breeze washed over them with a scent of coffee and gardenia. "How about you guys? We wanted to see a show this week, but between the high price tag and the baseball tickets we already bought, it didn't really pan out."

"Same," Spencer and Sakura said, also dissolving into bubbly giggles. "Maybe if we stare at our pictures of the sign for long enough, we can convince ourselves we saw it."

The blonde woman's phone started ringing, and after taking one quick but frustrated look, she turned to her friend.

"It's my sister. Do you mind if I—"

The other woman waved her off. "Go ahead. I'll wait here."

It didn't take an expert to surmise that the person in front of Spencer didn't come from a typically cold climate like San Francisco. Her friend was dressed like they were out on a casual stroll in the middle of summer, while she bundled up with her thick sweater and tights. The woman tightened her arms around her waist in the wake of another gust of wind, and as she yanked on the ends of her sweater in an attempt to shield herself from the city's low temperature, the gold Heritage Hawaiian bangle around her wrist caught Spencer's eyes. She absentmindedly spun it around while checking for any visual signs of concern from her friend. After seeing the other woman laugh while still speaking to her sister, her shoulders relaxed and she turned back to Sakura and Spencer.

"Feel free to tell me to fuck off but... you wouldn't happen to be from Hawai'i, are you?" Spencer asked.

Nothing excited a Hawai'i local more than running into another Hawai'i local while traveling. (Especially when they were Hawaiians.) Her eyes lit up with excitement, and she continued to relax more into the conversation.

"Yeah! Are you—"

"Just flew in from there on Sunday. Sakura—her—she lives here now but she's from Hawai'i too."

"That's so cool! I flew in on Sunday night too. We were probably on the same flight." She laughed.

Spencer liked the idea that someone else from home felt a calling to San Francisco, and in the same week no less.

"Is your friend from Hawai'i too?" Sakura asked.

"Oh, no," she answered, "Jordan's from Canada. Near Vancouver."

Ah. Spencer nodded. "That would explain the t-shirt." She paused. "'Cause she can stand the cold. Not 'cause of The Mummy."

"Well, Brendan Fraser is Canadian."

"So true. I hope they forgive me for forgetting." Spencer smiled. "Can I ask how you two—" She pointed back and forth between them.

"We met online, like, five years ago, maybe," the woman explained. "She's my best friend but it's our first time hanging out in person."

Sakura shifted on her feet which ended up with her leaning against Spencer's side, and warmth flooded her senses.

"That's so cool. How's your trip so far? Must've been a little nervous when you first got here."

"Oh, yeah." She nodded, hands resting on the long strap of her black crossbody bag. "I had a layover at LAX and I just sat there, worried that I wouldn't be as cool in person as she thought I was online. You know, nervous brain hard at work."

"Totally get it," Sakura said. "If it makes you feel any better, you don't at all look like you've just met met."

She smiled. Big and bright and free of any worry. The only way to exist while on vacation with a best friend.

"I'm glad." She laughed nervously. "She's saved my life, like, a hundred times since we became friends, so it would suck if we met and realized we weren't as compatible as we thought."

"Well, that's the cool part about meeting your person," Sakura said. "It doesn't matter how far apart you are or where life takes you. Every time you talk or see each other again it feels like coming home. Even if it's for the first time."

For as much flack as social media received, and though much of it was deserved, the ability of online spaces to connect people from different parts of the world, people who would otherwise never have crossed paths, allowed so many to grow a community beyond their immediate surroundings. That could never and should never be discounted.

Spencer and Sakura knew a thing or two about long-distance friendships. How uncontrollable space affected them. And yet, when push came to shove, they found their way back to each other. They needed a little time to find their footing and embrace the familiar rapport between them, but Spencer believed they were getting somewhere. As if coming back home after a long time away.

"Is this both of your first time here?" Spencer asked.

"It's my... fourth? I think... The last time was when I was 18. It's my favorite city in the entire world."

"Mine too." Sakura smiled. "You picked the perfect city to enjoy with her."

The blonde woman—Jordan—walked back like she knew they were talking about her. And like a true Canadian, the first words out of her mouth were an apology.

"I'm so sorry. My sister just got some news so she needed to scream about it. Anyway, Steph, when did you say that the next bus was coming?"

"Shit. Right. We should walk over." Steph turned back to them. "Sorry, we're directionally challenged so we have to find the right bus stop and hope we don't get lost. Again. But it was nice talking with you. Maybe we'll see each other on our flights back home." She laughed.

Sakura looped her arm through Spencer's. "Assuming I don't convince her to quit her job and stay here. She's already quit the man."

Jordan and Steph high-fived her for that one. Any other day and Spencer might have cried thinking about it again. But she was in good company, so she laughed along with them.

"Enjoy the rest of your day," Jordan said before waving. The two of them shuffled away, heads ducked together as they consulted with Google Maps. Just a couple of ladies on a mission.

Chapter 9

"How's your parents doing?" Sakura asked.

"They're alright, I guess," Spencer answered. "They're at that age when I'm starting to see how similar they are to my grandparents, and it's both hilarious and slightly terrifying."

The crowd levels of the farmers market were mild enough that it wasn't difficult to get around. Spencer was mostly just along for the ride since she didn't have groceries to buy, but she envied the price tag on all the produce that Sakura picked at from one booth to the next. San Francisco, like Hawai'i, was by no means cheap, as her bank account dwindled in pain and agony, but they had a lot of great and affordable options in that market. If she were a better cook, Spencer would have volunteered to make Sakura something nice before she left. Unfortunately, she would have to settle for taking her out to dinner or buying too many rounds of drinks at an overpriced bar. Whichever suited her friend's interest best.

"Oh, I totally get it." Sakura dropped a couple of grapefruit into her canvas tote. "Bachan came over to make soup the other week, and she and my mom were sitting together in the kitchen, playing their crosswords. God, they looked like twins. And not like in that adorable way you say about all parents and children. Like, actual twins. It was scary."

Spencer stepped closer to Sakura as the wind picked up around them. She had gotten used to that. Being so close to Sakura. And though she didn't call her out on it, Sakura always seemed to mirror her movements, ensuring that Spencer wasn't subjected to the unfamiliar cold weather.

The concept of time eluded her almost as much as the idea that she grew up a little more each day. Being there with her former best friend brought Spencer back to all the years they spent growing up, being girls and almost women together. But they were in San Francisco and they were now women, and that meant an inherent amount of change, not just in where they were but who they were. Back when they were younger, they went shopping together all the time. They walked around grocery stores and picked up various produce, pretending like they couldn't decide on what gourmet meal to prepare when they returned home. They laughed as they tried to pronounce the names of the more exotic varieties, and cackled when they got away with sneaking a grape or two from the bags in-store. But they don't do that now at 23. Not in a city miles and miles away from home. They don't hop on planes to see each other for a surprise weekend getaway.

Except that they apparently do. That week they did, anyway. Until they went back to not.

"And Morgan is doing alright?" Sakura asked after waiting too long for Spencer to say something.

"Yeah. She finally graduated last year. Goes to HPU now."

"Nice. You gotta give her a hug for me."

Spencer nodded. "'Course."

They stopped at Far West Fungi to pick up mushrooms for a mushroom and miso spaghetti recipe Sakura had seen online and wanted to try. The old man working the booth reminded her of her grandfather who passed away while she was in high school. All crinkled smiley eyes, a wide, toothy grin, and arms that looked perfect for hugging. More evidence of the passage of time and how it was equally terrifying as it was exciting. Maybe in another lifetime, Spencer could have been born in the quiet countryside where she could grow her crops and set up booths at the farmers market. She could run into strangers, strike up conversations with any friendly face in the crowd, and do it all over again the next day. She wouldn't be waiting on the edge of her seat to be rushed back to her regular boring life.

Spencer stopped to watch Sakura as she examined all of her options. The way her brows furrowed together, and her lips pursed in concentration. The crinkle on her forehead, strangely enough, reminded her once again of their younger years and how often she made that face.

"She's a thing of beauty, ain't she?"

She looked up at the booth attendee who was holding out a mushroom for Sakura to admire, eyes wide and full of pride over this tiny thing. They gushed over its wild shape and how great it tasted in pasta dishes, and he gave her more recommendations on different ways to cook it. Of course, he was friendly but also a great salesperson, and Sakura more than Spencer knew she needed for the spaghetti.

"Can I get you anything, hon?" he asked after finishing ringing up Sakura.

Spencer stopped, took a quick look around. She picked up a couple packs of dried mushrooms without thought and handed it over to him. Her mom could find some kind of use for them.

"Just these."

"Where are you from?"

"Hawai'i." She handed over a few bills. "That obvious?"

Of course, it was that obvious. But why did it matter? Why did she care whether she was from there? Probably because she knew enough of the San Francisco culture to not want to embarrass herself. Maybe also a bit of wondering how obvious it was that she had no sense of self, no idea where she fit in.

"You're not from here." He used a mushroom to point at Sakura. "She's from here, but not from here. You can probably read people like that at home, right?"

Spencer laughed. She supposed she could. Hawaiian. Kama'aina. Transplants (and other less savory labels that people freaked out over because it forced people to confront the role they played in illegal occupation). They were all different. It took her seconds to clock people back home. She knew this.

After completing the transaction, Spencer pocketed the dried mushrooms in Sakura's tote, and they returned to their leisurely stroll.

"Has he tried to contact you?" The brave question. Officially past the halfway mark of her trip, and this was the first time she asked about him so directly. She couldn't decide if that was pathetic, sad, or a little bit of both.

Then again, Spencer considered it progress that she didn't want to throw up over the question. "He emailed me last night."

"He emailed you?" Sakura gawked. "God, what year is he living in?"

Spencer couldn't help it. She laughed. "People still use email. Lots of people."

"Not couples. Ex-couples. They text and call like normal people."

"Or maybe they make grand romantic gestures and show up at the airport with a boombox and a dream." Spencer shrugged.

This time, they both laughed.

"Yeah, he's never been the grand romantic gesture type," Sakura said.

"He wouldn't have taken BART just to get me from the airport," Spencer joked.

Sakura flipped her hair. "Never give a man a job that you know a woman will get done so much better."

Spencer nodded. Gulped. Tightened her fingers around the strap of her purse.

"What did the email say?" Sakura expertly moved the conversation forward before Spencer could make a fool of herself.

"He wanted to make sure I got here okay." Her sister Morgan hadn't betrayed her, but she had let the news slip when he had showed up at the house looking for Spencer. If she thought about that too hard, Spencer would be left wondering if there was some kind of hope for their future. Maybe he cared. Maybe he cared more than he showed. But whenever those thoughts occurred, she quickly shifted back into her reminders that even if it were the truth, it came too late. "And he asked if we could talk when I got back."

She hadn't responded to her email yet. At some point, she would have to see him, but she had no idea when she would be ready for that.

"Oh," was all Sakura said.

Chapter 10

Spencer didn't know a thing about baseball.

She didn't understand sports in general as someone who didn't find them that interesting and didn't regularly partake in physical activities herself, therefore found it exhausting to watch. The only sport she occasionally watched was F1, and that only happened when she woke up in the middle of the night to find her sister curled up in front of the TV for a race happening halfway around the world. Spencer waited up with her for solidarity but always fell asleep before the chequered flag.

When Sakura surprised her that morning with tickets to see the Giants' opening game of the 2025 season, she was surprised by the genuine joy that rushed over her. If she had to be convinced to attend a sporting event, she preferred the idea of a baseball game over something like football. She imagined baseball fans to be slightly less... frightening.

"My friend and I went to the last Athletics game at the Coliseum last September," Sakura said while rummaging through her closet in search of Giants-appropriate attire. If Spencer had known they were going, she could have packed the singular orange t-shirt she owned. "It was so sad. You could tell how devastated everyone was. End of an era."

She leaned back for a moment, pointing at the pinboard hanging on the wall beside her. Spencer stood and walked over to see the FINAL GAME home plate pin sitting front and center, surrounded by various other pins. Elphaba and Glinda, pride flags, cable cars and Golden Gate Bridges, the Radish Spirit, Moana (many times), Stitch (many more times), and the Fellowship's Eleven leaf brooches, among many others.

The area around the board was where she tacked up a bunch of postcards. Not only one style or subject matter, but a true collage of all the interests that kept Sakura's heart beating. Spencer knew this would be something she missed most when she returned home, being able to wake up every morning, stop by this wall, and let something new catch her eye.

"Who are we playing today?" Spencer asked. As if she were part of San Francisco and not the mere guest she was.

"Seattle."

"... Seahawks?"

"Mariners." Sakura laughed.

"Close enough."

Sakura directed her to stand closer, and she alternated between two different options. Both were Giants-licensed merchandise. Both were perfectly acceptable, nondescript options that didn't require that kind of lingering consideration, yet Spencer stood there with Sakura deciding on which would look best, and she felt light and fluttery during every second of it.

"I've never been to Seattle," Spencer said after clearing her throat.

"You've never been to a lot of places," Sakura teased. She tossed the rejected shirt into a pile on the floor of her closet. "We should go some time. You'd love it. Beautifully green, freshest air. The Pacific Northwest is to die for. So many Hawaiians and other Pacific Islanders live there."

Spencer almost stopped herself from indulging in the idea that there isn't five years' worth of baggage between them but ultimately decided against it. If she wanted to pretend like this kind of spontaneous trip was a regular occurrence just to make it through whatever awaits her, she'll do it, and it'll feel good.

"I could probably do September," she said with a shrug.

"And I'll hold you to it."

Spencer spun around as quickly as she could move when Sakura started lifting her pajama shirt over her head without warning. She wore a bra underneath and it wasn't like they hadn't changed in front of each other before, having known each other for most of their lives, but she still kept her back to her. Spencer counted for three seconds, allowing her brain to stop running on overdrive, before following suit.

They turned back around once their baseball outfits were in place. Spencer looked like she was wearing a costume, while casually cool Sakura looked immaculate. Spencer didn't voice any of that thought because she knew Sakura would have scolded her for the unnecessary comparison. The picture-taking was her progress for the week. Spencer didn't want to push it.

"Ready to go?" Sakura clipped her carabiner hooked to her keys onto her left belt loop.

Ignoring the weight of this being the penultimate day of her San Francisco trip, Spencer nodded. The shirt smelled like Sakura, so Spencer smelled like Sakura.

"Ready," she confirmed.

Sakura stopped Spencer by the front door to adjust the clip holding her bangs back. She returned the favor as they were matching.

She couldn't remember who smiled first, but soon they were holding hands and walking out the door together. Like old times, except not.

"I went to one UH baseball game and it was so hot, I thought I was gonna get eaten by vultures."

Sakura stared at her, biting her lip.

"They were regular birds, obviously—"

"Whatever regular birds means."

"—and I also wasn't a decaying carcass. But you couldn't convince me that they weren't circling above, just waiting for me to die."

They stood in a long line stretched all the way back at a gate overlooking the water. Thankfully, neither of them brought bags so they didn't have to worry about checking them in for the duration of the game. People huddled together in their groups, awaiting entrance to their nighttime festivities. Despite not being a sports person, Spencer was excited to see the Giants play. Sakura seemed mildly interested enough, both due to her ownership of their Giants gear and the way her eyes kept bouncing around, taking everything in.

"When did you get into baseball?" Spencer asked.

"I'm bisexual, babe."

She shoved her. "You're a bisexual who played the trumpet and did color guard during marching band season because you were scared you'd trip and somehow choke on your mouthpiece."

Sakura hid behind her smile rather poorly. "A rational fear, I think."

"As rational as being scared of vultures feasting on me in Hawai'i. You're not a baseball bisexual," Spencer said matter-of-factly.

Sakura stepped forward as the line began to move; the gates had opened. "I could be. Maybe I already am."

This time, Spencer stopped and stared.

"Fine." Sakura huffed. "If you must know... I was dating this girl who liked baseball."

"Oh? And where is she now?"

Sakura hooked her arm with Spencer's. "Quit her too. Started a new routine."

"That's too bad."

"Not really." Sakura shrugged. "She sucked. I still get great tickets. Win, win."

Spencer searched her brain for something to say but came up empty. Was she supposed to console her? Say sorry? She made no indication of how recent this failed relationship was, or whether she was also currently nursing a broken heart because of it. Maybe she needed to be better about asking questions herself instead of wallowing in her misery.

An ugly cartoon crab stared down at her from one of the food stalls on the upper level.

Spencer rolled her eyes at it. Crazy Crab.

Once inside, the line dispersed enough to see more than a few inches in front of them. They had more than enough time to explore the ballpark at their own pace. The first order of business was taking pictures in front of the Giants logo not far from the entrance. Someone had even offered to take one of them together, sun shining right in their eyes and their arms wrapped around each other's shoulders. The pictures came out nice; how happy they made Spencer was even better.

Compared to the Aloha Stadium back home, which had been condemned around the time Sakura moved away and was slated to be demolished later that year, Oracle Park looked like Disney World. It had different areas to play games and breathtaking views over the water. It even had a cable car that patrons were allowed to hop on, which let Spencer take even more pictures.

On the way to their seats, they made a pit stop for hot dogs. Because a major league baseball game was not complete with the classic hot dog experience.

"Can I swap out for garlic fries too, please," Spencer said at the counter.

Sakura pulled out her wallet. "And she'll take the souvenir cup as well. Thank you."

"Oh, you don't have to—"

Spencer reached for her purse, but Sakura swatted her hand away. The cashier looked on at them, unamused, and stuck their hand out after repeating an astronomical total for the amount of food they had ordered.

"On me tonight," she said.

"But you bought the tickets," Spencer whined.

"How about... you buy me a drink later then, huh?" Sakura smiled.

Well, when she put it that way. That smile and a drink. Spencer couldn't say no to that.

Chapter 11

Even after four innings, Spencer still didn't know a thing about baseball.

"Raley, you bum! My grandmother runs faster than you and she's been dead for 15 years!"

Sakura tried her best to explain everything as it happened, including the most entertaining sport of home fans heckling the opposing outfield players—and to be honest, baseball wasn't a fast-moving sport so she had plenty of time to explain—but Spencer might as well have been the child left behind. Nothing stuck. The same type of play required multiple coachings, and she was still left confused. She kind of liked that, though. It meant she could keep leaning over to ask questions. Sakura always smiled, shook her head, and met her the rest of the way to reeducate her on the ins and outs of major league baseball.

"What's the matter with Raley?"

"He's a bum! He's a bum! He's a bum!"

"You must have really liked her," Spencer said.

Sakura turned away from the field. The next Giants player marched up to the plate. San Francisco was down one; both teams had scored a home run, but Seattle had an extra runner on the field for theirs giving them the score advantage.

"Huh?"

"The girl you started watching baseball for."

"What do you mean?"

Spencer shifted her legs toward Sakura to avoid getting popcorn thrown on her from someone above. "As established earlier, you are not a baseball bisexual, yet you know enough that I bet you could go down there and stand your own next to those coaches."

Maybe she was exaggerating. Maybe she simply believed that no matter how qualified, Sakura could do anything she put her mind to.

"That's just my air of women-are-better-than-men."

"So, it stands to reason that you must have really liked her. You wouldn't have taken all that time learning about it if you didn't."

As boldly as Sakura lived, she loved between the lines. She left Hawai'i a single woman, but her last relationship before the move had lasted a year and a half. The longest of them all at the time. While classmates posted sappy captions under a staged picture for every monthiversary, Sakura posted candids of her partner smiling unknowingly for the camera; a picture placed snugly between other aesthetically pleasing photos of her week. She packed their favorite Hawaiian Sun juice every day for lunch, always with an ice pack kept in her lunch box. When she picked up her partner from their house, their favorite playlist was already playing before they sat in the passenger seat. And every present included an annotated book using highlighters and post-its of their favorite color.

If Sakura spent all that time learning and falling in love with a new sport she previously had no interest in, it mattered.

Sakura licked her lips before glancing down at her lap. "I think I just... I think I liked the idea of her more than who she actually was. I mean, I know that. Like I said, she sucked. It was good that I moved on from her."

"When did you figure it out?"

"Hey, Raley! Your mom told me you're her least favorite player!"

"Much earlier than I left." Sakura laughed.

Spencer didn't like that answer.

The Giants player's bat connected with the ball and sent it flying across the field. They sprinted to first base with ease, and the ballpark erupted into applause while

Sakura remained still. The most calm and unmoving she had been the entire night.

"Maybe I was lying a little bit earlier. Or, well, not lying, but not being completely honest. It took me a long time to get used to the city. It feels very similar to Hawai'i in the way that there's the heart of the city through which you find the people with a strong sense of community, and then there are those loud groups who seek to rob it of what makes it unique and beautiful. It took me a long time to get comfortable enough here that I wasn't constantly checking flights back home. I thought I'd cave and go crawling back. But I jumped into a relationship with the first person who didn't make me feel like I was wearing clown makeup every day. And hey, it was nice for a while. She tethered me to this city enough to hold my head up. I thought that if I let her go, it would somehow curse this city for me. Like I'd never succeed here, you know? It's stupid."

Spencer shook her head. "Don't say that. It's not."

"Eventually I realized she liked me not for me but because I was easy to manipulate. I was new, lost, still figuring out who I was. She took advantage of that, even if it meant making me feel small so she could hold herself up higher. Above me. Always above me. It's the worst feeling—thinking you're holding onto someone when they're really holding you down."

Spencer regretted pushing the issue. Not because she didn't want to hear it, but because every honest word that poured out of her friend's vulnerability burned like the familiar sting of a shot of hard liquor she knew she didn't enjoy but drank anyway.

"Actually," Sakura continued, "the worst is when you figure out it's happening but you're too scared to let go. 'Cause then that means having to commit to figuring out how to stand on your own two feet."

Spencer nodded. "Yeah. Yes."

Her boyfriend hadn't gotten along with her best friend, even though they technically knew each other first. Once upon a time, they were friends. The kind of friends that hung out at lunch and grouped themselves together for school projects. They weren't friendly outside of those scenarios, though. Spencer thought it was a good thing they knew each other. Once they started dating, that meant her two favorite people already had a rapport. The three of them would be inseparable.

But, of course, life didn't work that way. Some people were only meant to be friends in very limited capacities. Once they all started hanging out together outside of school, the friendship between Sakura and him deteriorated past the point of no return.

"He's awful to you. You do realize that, right?" Sakura packed up her things having already declared the planned sleepover to be canceled. "I'm so tired of shitty guys getting away with bottom-of-the-barrel behavior and girls just fawning over them. You're better than that."

"Well, maybe I'm not." Spencer inconspicuously wiped away any tears threatening to fall. "Maybe he's the only kind of guy out there who will give me the time of day. I'm not like you, okay, Sakura? People fall at your feet—guys, girls, even freaking parents—"

"Oh, god. Don't do that. Don't make me out to be this mystical creature. It's demoralizing."

"They all love you. He's the only guy who's ever looked in my direction. I'm sorry, okay?"

Sakura stopped, turning slowly. Her hair was piled haphazardly on top of her head, her shirt wrinkled, her sad and dull eyes, and her patience wearing thin. The most embarrassing part was that this hadn't been the first time they engaged in this topic of conversation. How awful he was. How she forgave him. How she wanted better for her.

"There's a whole world out there of amazing people who would treat you the way you should be treated. People who would make sure you treat yourself the way you should be treated. And it breaks my heart every time I see you forget that."

Sakura left before Spencer could formulate a response. A text from him arrived precisely as the front door shut, and Spencer managed to ignore it for the night. Her overwhelming need to feel like she was the bigger person made her reply the next morning, though, which didn't fill the empty space left behind in Sakura's absence.

"Raley, you bum! I bet you hit reply-all to company-wide emails!"

The fourth inning ended. Each screen lit up with colorful graphics, and fans around the ballpark rose from their seats in haste for a quick purchase before the game started back up again.

Spencer hugged the Giants hoodie she had purchased earlier a little closer. "The whole world is out there waiting for you. You'll find someone."

They smiled at each other in the middle of Oracle Park.

"Alright, folks! As voted by all of you here with us tonight and at home, please join us for a sing-along of your favorite still going strong from this summer! It's time for Hot To Go! by Chappell Roan!"

Sakura and Spencer immediately jumped to their feet as the first beats of Hot To Go! rolled in. Their worlds had both seemingly shattered, in different places and at different times, but maybe they didn't need the whole world. Maybe this city was enough, especially when they were both in it together.

They sang along to the lyrics, loudly and proudly. Some people joined in around them, others stared. It didn't matter when they were lost in each other, the song, and San Francisco. They bumped their hips together and giggled, all while pledging to move on from the people who took everything and gave them nothing.

Chapter 12

The Giants lost.

Spencer still had fun. She decided she needed to learn how to do that more—go along for the ride, even if she had no idea where she was going, and enjoy herself. Despite the loss, Sakura didn't seem bummed either. She linked their hands together on the way out to ensure they didn't get separated, and once they were back outside, they remained connected, arms swinging back and forth with each step.

Sakura directed her to the Willie Mays statue out front for pictures. On the way, they passed countless hot dog vendors with the divine fragrant aroma of sauteed onions and peppers. If she wasn't still full from the hot dog, garlic fries, three beers, and ice cream sundae in a mini souvenir helmet, she might have been tempted to try it at least once.

It took them some time to get a good shot of the statue. It was late, which didn't help, and a lot of people weaved their ways through the crowd. Spencer recognized the name but didn't know much about him. While Sakura took pictures, she read up about him on her phone.

"Where do we have to walk to?" Spencer asked once Sakura returned, satisfied.

She pointed her finger at the same station they arrived at. "Lucky us, we don't have to walk to the Caltrain station."

Maybe it was all the beer she had drunk—it might have been more than three, she couldn't remember—but Spencer didn't want to go home just yet. The night seemed so young, and they didn't have much time left, so she wanted to prolong it as much as possible. She knew the second they entered Sakura's apartment, the undeniable dread of having to say goodbye again would creep up until eventually becoming unavoidable.

"Is it okay if we get home late?" Spencer asked.

Sakura tightened her grip around Spencer's fingers.

"Yeah. Sure. Let's walk," she added, as if reading her mind.

As late and dark as it was, the streets around Oracle Park were busy enough that Spencer didn't feel nervous. Truthfully, most of San Francisco felt safe to her by any metropolitan standards. San Francisco got a bad rep that it didn't deserve. Spencer knew a lot of it simply had to do with certain groups trying to demonize "liberal" cities and states. The wealthy, privileged, and more fortunate preferred to vilify those less fortunate than them instead of criticizing the government for failing to do its job, or the individualistic nature of society at large in the United States of America. People wanted the cozy comfort of existing in a community without putting in the effort of actively and meaningfully participating in said community. They would rather type away furiously on a keyboard about how someone living on the street, through no choice of their own, was such an inconvenience rather than look them in the eyes and smile. A reminder that they were all human was too steep a price to pay when the machine needed to keep moving.

"I think we can officially call you a baseball bisexual," Spencer declared as they strolled down King Street.

Sakura raised her chin with a smile. "The best of the best."

"I think you're doing alright," Spencer said, looking forward. "More than alright. You seem so... happy. Yourself."

"Thank you."

"It makes me feel weirdly better about..." Spencer stopped before finishing her sentence. Probably shouldn't have started it in the first place.

"Better about... ?" Sakura trailed off.

Spencer shrugged and let her hand slip away. "For not checking in this whole time."

The sound of Sakura's chunky boots stomping against the pavement halted.

"You didn't—" she started to say.

"There's no excuse. I was sad, and instead of unpacking my feelings and dealing with them, I shut myself off. It was shitty and you deserved a better friend, especially during such a new and challenging time in your life."

For years, Spencer chalked their relationship up to a victim of growing up. As if it were an unavoidable thing that happened. The truth came with more accountability; Spencer allowed their friendship to deteriorate, just as she had allowed her relationship to deteriorate. Granted, one of those deserved it since it was built on an already rocky foundation. But she still needed to own up to her actions.

"You know, I never read that letter you sent me," Spencer said after a few beats of silence.

Sakura's jaw dropped for a few seconds like she had seen a ghost. A letter long forgotten by that point.

It arrived two months after Sakura settled into her new city. Spencer remembered it clearly, even as it sat untouched at the back of her closet. The envelope was pale blue with a stamp of the Golden Gate Bridge. She recognized the handwriting before reading what it said. A stick sealed on the back sealed the flap. She hadn't immediately dumped it into her closet. No, she sat with it for days like a weight in her hands. Tempted by what could be inside but too afraid to expose herself to some-thing that could potentially rip her heart open, inten-tionally or not. One afternoon as she debated reading it, he barreled into her house unannounced, and she ran faster than she had ever moved to hide it from him. He remained blissfully unaware; Spencer dreaded knowing of its existence.

"You—" Sakura sat down on the stairs leading up to some store. The CLOSED sign hung in the window. "You don't have to read things you aren't ready for. I don't—you shouldn't feel bad. It was something I should have said before I left, anyway."

Spencer didn't ask her what was in the letter. It didn't seem fair when she knew she was leaving soon.

"I think we both did some things we knew we shouldn't have," Sakura continued. "I don't know if it makes sense to dwell on them now."

"But shouldn't we? Not dwell on them but... I don't know, resolve whatever happened before?"

Sakura tapped the spot next to her. They sat with enough space between them that it allowed Spencer to breathe and think straight. The years pounded down on them like a storm after a long drought. She rested her chin on the palm of her hand instead of picking at her cuticles. Quietly, they allowed a group of people to pass with all of their baseball gear and jovial spirits.

"We were young, silly girls. I don't want to burden our current selves with the mistakes those girls made. Do you?"

Spencer closed her eyes and sighed. Nodded a confirmation to Sakura and then herself.

"I don't know if I would've said yes if the situations were reversed," Spencer admitted, and it felt terrible to do so. With the past few days in her rearview mirror, of course she could say at that moment that she would have let Sakura spend the week with her if she had called her randomly on a Saturday night. But she had no idea if that was the truth. If she would have proved to be the same coward that didn't open that letter years ago. "I wouldn't have been mad if you said no, honestly."

Sakura shook her head. "Of course, I wouldn't have. Doesn't matter what's happened between us or how long it's been. You'll always have a room in my home."

Home. San Francisco, not Hawai'i.

"Here or there," Sakura added. The fucking incredible woman who knew Spencer better than she knew herself most days. Most years. Most lifetimes.

"We were eating at the Makiki Zippys," Spencer said, her eyes already beginning to well up with tears. "It was late. I think we went to a concert or something, but we got into an argument before we left the house, so neither of us was in the mood. We ended up leaving early to get something to eat. I wanted Taco Bell, he wanted Zippys, so, you know."

Sakura shook her head. "That prick."

"It was completely empty. And, well, I guess I'm the world's worst judge of when to say something serious, so I opened up to him about something I had been thinking about for years. I thought... I don't know, I thought he would understand or try to understand. Maybe I subconsciously knew that he wouldn't but I hoped that he would. He was my fucking boyfriend. He's supposed to care about me and what I'm struggling with. But he didn't."

The most embarrassing part about the story she was telling was how long the relationship lasted after it happened. Spencer's stomach curdled at the thought of it, of how fucking tragic and mortified she was to admit any of this to someone, even though she knew Sakura, of all people, would never judge her for a moment. Maybe it was because she knew Sakura would have never found herself in that situation, and if she had, she would have been brave enough to leave.

Or maybe she wouldn't have, Spencer wondered after hearing her story earlier. Maybe they were alike in that way.

"I told him I liked girls, too. About how I had been struggling with hiding it for a long time. It wasn't like I was dying to tell him specifically. I just needed to tell someone, at least one person, or else I'd go mad. I still loved him. I wasn't looking at anyone or fooling around with anyone. I just... I needed that off my fucking chest, you know? It was just... eating away at me." Spencer wiped away snot and tears. "The first thing he did was ask me if I was fucking cheating on him. I just laughed 'cause I thought he was joking at first. But he kept getting angrier and angrier, and he didn't even believe me when I told him I wasn't. Why would you tell me that? Why does it matter if you like girls? You're with a guy. Like, I don't know, dude, maybe I'm being fucking vulnerable with you about a part of me I've never admitted to anyone else? But he kept getting mad, calling me names, telling me I'm disgusting for even saying—"

Spencer rubbed her shaking hands all over her face, smearing the tears around until she tasted salt on her lips.

"He called me a slut. Trashy. Gross. Said I was just looking for attention because we hadn't had sex in three months."

"Spencer—" Sakura, tearful herself, reached out a hand before pulling it back as Spencer curled in on herself. "You're not—you're none of those things. He's an asshole who needs to get his shit rocked and—"

"I wanted to feel normal. I wanted someone to tell me there was nothing wrong with me. Why do we stay with assholes like that? Because we don't know any better? Because we're weak? Because we're afraid of being alone more than we're afraid of being hurt? God, what is wrong with me?"

Sakura closed the distance between them with one gentle hand on either side of her face. With tears falling from her eyes, she forced Spencer to look at her. Her. No one else. No other vision in an otherworldly landscape. Spencer wanted to clasp their hands together, force them to never let go, but she dug her nails into her legs and wished for all of the angry voices in her head to go away.

"There is nothing wrong with you, okay? Nothing. You are strong. You are so strong, and so brave, and I'm so, so sorry that anyone ever made you feel otherwise. You didn't deserve that, okay? You deserve—" Sakura wrapped her arms around Spencer and held her so tightly that she didn't know where one person started and the other ended. "I love you. I'm so sorry. I love you and I'll always be here for you. I'm sorry that I wa—I love you."

Chapter 13

"Get dressed. We're going out tonight."

She just barely moved her head from her position lying down on the couch. They had scarfed their way through some of the best Chinese takeout she had ever eaten in her life, and she was too tired from their hike earlier to get started on packing all of her belongings. Her sluggish nature might have also had something to do with how she hated the idea that by this time tomorrow, all traces of her would be gone from the apartment.

Spencer didn't know what she was less ready for—leaving San Francisco or returning home.

"Where to?" she asked.

The shower started running. On My Side by Leighton Meester filled the apartment with beautiful, soothing, and perfectly upbeat sounds. Over the past week,

Spencer had memorized the scent of Sakura's strawberry and mint body wash. She closed her eyes, already anticipating the scent washing over her. She desperately needed a shower quickly if they were headed out for the night.

"It's a surprise."

Spencer didn't question it. She would follow Sakura on whatever path she set forth on tonight.

After swapping places so Spencer could take her shower, they both ended up crammed in the tiny bathroom. Makeup, skin care, and hair products were scattered across the counter, all mixed so Spencer couldn't remember which items belonged to who. Sakura didn't want to give any hints, so Spencer had to improvise with the safest style options for any possible occasion.

Spencer loved makeup, but she wasn't any good at putting it on. Some kind of disconnect between the vision in her head and the capabilities of her hands. Sakura let her try some of her products—newer, fancier, much more cared for than the stained and dirty compacts that occupied Spencer's makeup bag. She gravitated toward neutrals most days, but she dusted her cheekbones and collarbones with

Just before Spencer swiped on some gloss, Sakura brandished a gold tube of red lipstick. She walked behind Spencer, pulled her hair over her shoulders, and held the lipstick up to her face, testing the shade against her complexion.

"This would look so good on you."

Spencer shimmied away and grabbed the tube from her. Twisted the lipstick up and down, as if it would change the product itself.

"I don't look good in red lipstick."

"You've never tried red lipstick."

"You're drop-dead gorgeous. You'd look good in any lipstick shade."

Spencer blushed.

Sakura took the lipstick tube back and prepped her canvas—a dab of a tissue to absorb any excess lip balm, the tiniest swipes of lip liner at the perimeter of her lips, her thumb resting gently on her chin. She applied the lipstick in thin layers that she built up a few times, blotting in between. By the time Spencer looked at her reflection in the mirror, the red lipstick blurred softly around the edges like a stain. As if she had spent the entire afternoon eating berries and drinking wine.

"Told you you'd look good." Sakura peeked over her shoulder with a glossy smile of her own. Her warm eyes were rimmed with smoky tones, contrasting Spencer's style for the night.

Spencer wanted to tell her she looked beautiful, too, but the words got stuck in her throat. A message in a bottle swept up and lost in the currents. Sakura disappeared into another area of the apartment, leaving Spencer to wonder what kind of mark she would leave behind if she kissed her cheek.

Sakura opened the door for her.

"You brought me to... a karaoke bar?"

The green sign outside read THE MINT, while the smaller red sign directly beneath read KARA. A rainbow pride flag hung from the front of the bar. Colorful fairy lights were strung up around the entire room. She spotted at least five carabiners within seconds of walking inside. The person monitoring the front door called her darling. Spencer felt immediately comforted despite the crowdedness of the bar.

"I used to come here a lot when I first got into the city," Sakura explained as they weaved through swaying bodies to find a table. "It's decently cheap. And I like that everyone is all here together. Not separated in their little rooms, you know?"

The stage came into view once they managed to snag an open table. It was small enough not to look so intimidating but big enough to command the attention of the entire bar. Two people danced under the spotlights, singing along to a song that Spencer vaguely recognized enough to remember she had heard it in Coyote Ugly, but not enough to know the name.

"Can we get the usuals, Needy?" Sakura requested a random person wandering past their table.

They were dressed in all black casual attire with a white bar map tucked over their waistband. The only obvious sign that they worked there since they weren't carrying anything in their hands. "I'm not a damn server, Sakura."

"No, but you're already up. Might as well make yourself useful." Her tone was playful, lighthearted. They talked like old friends.

The person twirled around on their heel, ready to dig into Sakura's request, before their eyes landed on Spencer. For a moment, they stared at each other. And then they smiled like they were the bearer of the world's greatest secret.

"Oh, this is the one?"

Sakura, to Spencer's surprise, blushed. "Um, this is—"

"Spencer. Right." They held out their hand. "Nice to finally meet you. I'm Needy."

"Finally?" She didn't want to think about the implications of their word choice, but she couldn't help herself. "Nice to meet you too, Needy."

"Finally. She hasn't shut up about you since she got here. I'll be right back with your drinks."

They took off for the bar, leaving Sakura and Spencer to sit awkwardly together and wait.

Spencer couldn't remember the last time she went to a karaoke bar. She didn't sing well to begin with, let alone in front of other people. If she did, it was because there was a good chance she was drunk. Patron after patron cycled through their chance to shine on stage, and they cheered for each of them through sips of their drinks.

"Have you ever gone up?" Spencer asked.

Sakura looked at her, raised a brow, and threw her head back with a soft laugh. "Only when I'm drunk."

"And what's your song of choice?"

She gave it some thought. "Mr. Brightside."

"Mr. Brightside?" Spencer scoffed. As if that song wasn't in her top ten every single year. "How original."

Sakura smacked her arm. "Karaoke songs are sup- posed to be classics! How can you expect everyone to sing along if they don't know the words?"

"Fair enough."

When Spencer first got a fake ID, a friend from school took her to a bar downtown. She disliked it so much that it kept her away from bars for a long time. She could count on one hand the number of times she visited another. It had nothing to do with that particular bar itself. Spencer struggled with visits to certain places. She spent too much time worrying about whether she fit in or if everyone else was secretly judging her. Most of it was in her head, of course, but recognizing that was easier than knowing how to handle it.

None of that unease transferred here. She took her jacket off and hung it on the back of her chair. Let her hair down despite its current poofy state. Kept the drinks flowing. And not once did she worry about what some stranger in that bar thought about her, or whether anyone was thinking about her at all.

"Needy was one of the first friends I made here," Sakura explained. The friend in question stood behind the bar now, making drinks. People smiled, laughed, and enjoyed their company. "Actual friend. Not just someone I hung out with because I didn't know anyone else." A big, significant difference. "I thought I knew what it meant to be bisexual. Queer. But there's a difference between being part of the LGBTQ community and being queer. Being gay or bisexual or anything else under the umbrella, it's something you're born with. An identity that no one can take away from you. But being queer is more than an identity. It's a political movement. It means doing the work—dismantling harmful systems and fighting for equality, not just for ourselves but for others. Needy's been really helpful in that regard, teaching me how to be queer."

Spencer nodded. In truth, she still felt like an outsider looking in fondly through the frosted window. So brand new to the idea of accepting herself as she was in her heart. But she felt the inside of her chest slowly warming with each passing moment, thawing from freezing herself out of the freedom to be who she always knew she was. A realization as freeing as it was frightening.

She had so much to learn about the world waiting there at her fingertips.

Sakura squeezed her hand underneath the table. "You don't have to struggle trying to fit yourself into another box. That's the beauty of being queer. The world is forever changing, forever growing, and so does our understanding of it. You don't need to get everything right the second you step outside. You just need to be open to learning."

Spencer nodded, thankful that, of all people, Sakura was the person holding her hand for the ride.

"Spencer Pelekai? Up next!"

Her eyes widened.

Sakura held up her hands. "Not me. I swear."

Across the bar, Needy smiled down at the drink they were making.

"Well..."

The last thing she wanted to do was keep this crowd waiting. They had all been such good sports so far. The show must go on.

Fueled by alcohol and good vibes, Spencer dusted herself off and made her way toward the stage. The attendant waiting nearby asked for her song selection. She froze, trying to think of what to sing. Mr. Brightside came to mind, but she wanted to save that for when she signed Sakura up later. If she was going to potentially embarrass herself, she needed to do so with a bang. The ultimate crowd pleaser.

She pulled up Spotify and the last song she listened to stood out to her. Perfect.

Spencer informed the employee of her choice and earned a thumbs up in response. "First time tonight. Probably not the last."

"Hopefully not."

Piano notes fluttered through the air. Spencer stepped up to the plate, spotlight burning through years of a hardened shell. Sakura held her fingertips against her lips, trying to hide her smile. The crowd cheered her on.

"I know you wanted me to stay—"

It all happened in a flash, though Spencer would have been thrilled to spend forever in that moment. She didn't register her feet moving or her arms swinging or her voice rising without cracking. Pink Pony Club brought The Mint to its feet. Spencer didn't know what to do with that kind of attention, but quickly realized that she didn't really need to. That's what it meant to live in the moment.

At the end of the song, Spencer took a bow. As she stood, she beamed at the crowd with tears falling from her eyes. Needy ran over to hug her. She had never felt more alive in her life.

Sakura stood in the crowd clapping. "That's my girl!" she yelled.

Chapter 14

The world didn't end when Spencer's heart broke into two.

The truth was more complicated than that. It had shattered beyond recognition, but it was never the result of the end of a seven-year-long relationship with a man. It also had everything to do with her best friend, her former best friend, the woman standing in front of her in that tiny apartment in San Francisco. It had everything to do with still being afraid to come out to her family, even her beloved sister, who she ultimately knew would never seek to harm her. Her heart broke a million different ways throughout life through the simple virtue of being a queer woman of color navigating a world dominated by those who hated her existence. Born from a people who had their land, their rights, and their identity stripped from them, forced to fight for scraps in the small slivers of hope left behind. For Spencer to live and breathe was to persevere, no matter how unsteady her feet may be.

Cities were often like living, breathing human beings, too. They bore their own characteristics and forged unique relationships with everyone who visited. As much as San Francisco came to her by way of Sakura, Spencer and San Francisco grew to become kindred spirits. She had no idea when she would return and get to walk these streets again, and the undeniable pain of it being her last night in the city pained her.

Sakura stood in the kitchen with a kettle on the stove. She had washed her face clean of makeup and changed into comfy pajamas while Spencer desperately searched for the will to remove herself from the cough. The effort only marginally sustained her rather than allow her to succumb to the drowsiness induced by Sakura's humming.

"I don't want to go home," Spencer groaned—eyes closed, arms dangling over the carpet, and her head angled just perfectly toward her friend in the kitchen. Her bags had been packed in haste, aside from anything she needed in the morning, so she didn't have the excuse of needing to be productive to keep her going. It also, unfortunately, meant she couldn't delude herself into thinking she had more time left. "I could stay here forever."

She couldn't. She would miss Hawai'i too much not to return. But she loved the idea of staying there forever.

Sakura went uncharacteristically quiet under the guise of making her favorite nighttime tea. She was quiet even on the drive home, leaving Spencer to giggle with herself about the experience of riding in a Waymo for the last time.

She had nothing else to do. And, quite frankly, she wasn't sure what else in the world she was supposed to want to do. Spencer tugged the throw blanket off the back of the couch and draped it across her shoulders before sliding into the kitchen. Sakura didn't turn around upon her entrance, but her humming briefly paused in acknowledgment. Spencer interpreted this as a silent approval for her to sit on the counter on the opposite end of the kitchen. Not that there was much room to start with, but it gave the illusion of space.

Then again, did they need any more space between them than what already existed?

"You really don't have to take off work tomorrow, too, you know." Spencer's flight left early in the morning, which meant tonight was more or less all they had left. It seemed silly for her to take an entire day off just to drop her off at the airport before the sun was even up. "I can get to the airport by myself if it's easier."

Sakura shook her head. "Nonsense. I'll drop you off. It's the least I could do."

She was alluding to it as an exchange to how Spencer took her to the airport all those years ago, but Sakura didn't want to accept that she had done far more for her by letting Spencer not only crash at her place for the past week, but also showing her around the city the way only someone who loved it could.

With all the gentleness and forgiveness that someone who loved her could.

"You've... been a lifesaver this week. Thank you."

Spencer wanted to look at Sakura's face and decipher all the intricate emotions woven into every microexpression. The sharp edges of her cheekbones and the soft glimmer of her eyes. Even the red stain of her lips from biting it too hard when she thought no one else was looking. But, of course, Spencer saw. She saw everything, even the parts of her that she never knew existed. She didn't know of a time without Sakura, even if the only version she had was the ghost left behind during those five years spent apart.

"Any time." She finally turned around with two mugs in her hands. Steam rose from them as she handed one off to Spencer. "Any time while I'm still here, I guess."

Spencer took some time to formulate a response, thanks to the hot chocolate. "Are you planning on leaving?"

She hoped she didn't sound too disappointed or excited. On one hand, she would be thrilled to have Sakura back in Hawai'i, but she also didn't know if that would unearth emotions she wasn't ready to handle. Spencer had also gotten so used to the union of Sakura and San Francisco—and, to a different extent, Spencer and San Francisco—that she didn't want to think about what it meant for them to not be around anymore. Spencer knew she would eventually return to San Francisco one day. She hoped Sakura would be there to give her somewhere to land and feel like her home away from home.

"One day." Sakura shrugged. "I know this city, but I'm not of this city. I hope one day soon that it can be returned to those born and raised in it. The people who built it into the incredible place it is today. You know?"

"Yeah. I get that."

More silence fell upon them, cradled by the fragility of their week coming to an end. Spencer couldn't decide if it was better or worse that she had only planned on staying there for a week. Whether it was better that it didn't last long enough to get too comfortable, or if it needed to be longer to make up for all the time lost.

"Did you decide what you're going to do when you get home?" Sakura asked, her eyes turned down to the drink in her hands. She was so effortlessly beautiful in a way that people spent hours trying to achieve. The kind of beauty that others couldn't decide whether they were more jealous or admiring.

Spencer felt braver than normal. She didn't approach people first. She sulked along the edges until someone with more courage pulled her into the center with them. That was how she ended up in a seven-year-long relationship with someone who wasn't right for her. He pulled her out of her shell during a time in her life when she needed him, and she was too scared once she figured out that she needed to step out of her comfort zone.

Yet there she stood. More at ease than she could ever remember in her life, and that was not by coincidence. That light, airy feeling in her chest was because of a decision she had made for herself and because of the woman standing in front of her. A woman who was once girls with her.

"I'll probably call him one day. If I'm ever ready. We'll see."

Sakura nodded. "Well, whether you are or you aren't—and there's no right or wrong answer here—I 'll... I'm here for you."

Softly, carefully, Spencer reached her hand out to tuck her hair behind Sakura's ear. Sakura swallowed, not quite moving away or closer. And then, almost imperceptibly, she leaned ever so slightly into her hand with eyes closed. Lost in a daydream from years ago.

"If I asked you to tell me what was in that letter, would you?" Spencer asked.

Sakura quickly shook her head, and she felt her stomach sink before the explanation quickly followed. "I spent days working on it. Writing, rereading it, rewriting it. Scratching everything out before starting all over again. If I tried to recite that mess from memory, it wouldn't live up to it."

"You said it was something you should have said before you left, right?"

Sakura nodded.

"So, why didn't you?" Spencer probably didn't have the right to demand such answers, but she wanted them regardless. Would San Francisco have had any purpose at all if she had left without them? "You're always so good at putting yourself out there. Why didn't you—"

"You weren't really in a good place for me—" Sakura paused and stepped back. Her eyes remained closed. "We. We weren't really in a good place for it. It wouldn't have been fair."

"To who?"

"To you. To me." Quietly, she added, "To him."

The last admission came out like a bullet through an exit wound.

"You don't even like him," Spencer said.

"I did. At one point." Sakura paced through her kitchen under heavy observation—equal parts confusion, frustration, and fascination. "But, like most men in my life, he found a way to disappoint me. And, thanks to the other night, he hasn't stopped either."

But Sakura didn't hate him because she found out years later that he was biphobic and a general garbage excuse of a partner. Even if she didn't want to admit the real reason. Or maybe she had, and that admission was sitting on the floor in the back of Spencer's closet.

Spencer pushed aside her tea and slid off the counter. The blanket slipped away. Her nerves revved into overdrive. "Are we in a good enough place now to talk about it?"

"I don't know if that's a question for me to answer."

"Then can I ask you a question?"

She nodded.

Spencer stepped forward and, once again, rested her hand along the side of Sakura's face. "Is this okay?"

"Yes."

Women weren't mystical creatures. They were human beings anyone could understand, if only they remembered to listen. In that apartment in Castro, Spencer thought she heard Sakura's heartbeat. Maybe it was all in her head. Or perhaps she was filling in the gaps from the fluttering pulse beneath her touch. It only seemed to race faster once their lips touched. Once upon a time, when Spencer first confronted the idea that she liked women, she wondered if it would feel monumentally different. She worried if it would be obvious that she had far less experience with women. As if it mattered. As if that meant something. Because there was that box she was trying to place herself inside of. Another tool to restrict herself and the idea of her and what it meant to simply be.

Sakura leaned into the kiss with one hand pressed against the back of Spencer's head. If it felt like magic, it was because they left the idea of time behind. The years unraveled between them, burrowing into every kiss, every touch, every desperate breath of air. Where did Sakura start? Where did Spencer end? Where and how wholly did San Francisco embed itself into the fractured timeline of their togetherness?

How were they meant to let go tomorrow?

They had no idea.

Chapter 15

Spencer loved the San Francisco International Airport. Right now, she hated it.

A week ago, she had no idea what San Francisco would come to mean to her. She had no expectations. No real plans. Everything had unraveled as a complete surprise, down to the very last night. But Spencer still felt fulfilled by the experience, and she was grateful for the chance to escape from her real life, even if only for a week.

Sakura squinted up at the screen, verifying the correct gate. Even Spencer, a far less traveled person, knew the app was more handy. But she liked watching her, so she didn't mind waiting.

This airport drop-off felt much different than the last one for many reasons, most of which they didn't need to get into. The intimacy of getting undressed in front of someone new didn't alter the dynamic the way Spencer thought it would have, especially considering their long history. A blessing she wouldn't turn away. But they both seemed to adhere to a silent understanding that they weren't jumping into something so quickly without handling everything else going on in their lives. They weren't going back to being just friends. For now, they would take their time to figure it out.

"All checked in?" she asked.

Spencer nodded, yanking the backpack strap higher up on her shoulder. "Do upgrades always cost that much? Absurd."

"And to think... you're still gonna get served that shitty Hot Pocket knock off." Sakura pulled out a small paper bag from inside her tote and handed it over. The shape of the contents was unmistakable, along with the smell. Spencer hadn't noticed her making it that morning. "Spam musubis for the road. Or... for the skies, I guess."

In another lifetime, they knew nothing of goodbyes or long distances. In every other lifetime, they only knew forever.

Back in the heart of Castro, on top of Sakura's dresser, sat an unopened letter. Spencer had scribbled it in the middle of the night, not allowing herself to rethink every word or wonder if it made sense. They understood each other in the simplicity of one look across the room. Whatever poured out of her heart and onto that piece of paper would always make sense to Sakura. She knew this. She felt it.

The rest of the airport slipped away into nothingness. Sakura and Spencer embraced in a way that didn't exist five years ago. They clung to each other desperately, without reservation. Life didn't always make sense, but they would. The way they felt about each other would. If their love had been pulled straight out of folklore, their statues would appear exactly as they were now—two lovers wrapped up in each other moments before being forced apart. And if they were something slightly less grand but more touchable, they would be background characters in someone else's photograph, a story for strangers to discuss around the dinner table. Who were those women? Were they crying? Where were they from? Or going? Were they in love?

"I love you."

"I love you. Thank you for everything."

"Have a safe flight. Call me when you get home."

Sakura and Spencer. A little. Hawai'i, and sometimes San Francisco. Home. Yes.

Later, while sitting at an empty table waiting for boarding to start and eating an overpriced breakfast burrito, Spencer cried. Most of it was happy, but a lot of it was sad. She had arrived at the airport early enough that it wasn't busy, but people still walked past every now and then. She didn't think much of what others might have thought. She wasn't the first person to cry in an airport, and she wouldn't be the last.

Once the alert came through that boarding was about to begin, Spencer accepted that she was ready to go home.

Epilogue

Nowhere else in the world brought her to life like O Hawai'i nei. But San Francisco came pretty close.

As much as she missed what she was leaving behind in the city by the bay, and that feeling would only continue to grow with each passing day, she felt a calm relief wash over her once she stepped foot back home. Everything wasn't right in the world, and maybe the search for such certainties was a fallacy, but she would always feel right in Hawai'i. That would never change. That could never be taken from her.

"Oh, hey!" Someone pulled up beside her next to the baggage carousel. Stephanie, the woman from outside Orpheum Theater. She looked as tired as Spencer, and with an equal longing for some of the San Francisco chill in the air. "Good flight?"

"Good." Spencer nodded. She didn't even need to try and sound convincing because she spoke the truth. "Great. You?"

"Got a whole row to myself," Stephanie boasted.

She laughed. "Nice."

"So," Stephanie watched as the conveyor belt started to move, "was San Francisco everything you wanted it to be?'

It took her a second to reply. Not because she didn't know the answer. Spencer fully settled into San Francisco being a past and not the present.

"Everything and more."

Spencer and Stephanie briefly talked while waiting for their bags to come around. (Spencer had splurged by paying to check her suitcase.) (If by splurge she meant that her bag was overweight from too many Trader Joe's snacks and omiyage for friends and family.) When the time came for them to part after their serendipitous run-in, they exchanged social media handles before saying their goodbyes. Stephanie walked away with a brand new friendship bracelet on her wrist—a baseball glove charm on one side and a seashell on the other.

"Welcome back, beloved sister. Your chariot awaits."

Morgan leaned back against the passenger door of her car, ignoring the scowl directed at her from the airport attendant.

"God, I missed you." Spencer, despite being taller, collapsed into Morgan's arms.

"I missed you too," Morgan echoed. They squeezed each other tightly before finally letting go. Morgan reached for the discarded bags. "How was your flight?"

Spencer didn't want to bore her sister with curbside pleasantries. They had a whole Sunday to themselves to laugh and cry and reminisce.

"Wanna sleep over? I'll tell you all about it."

Morgan loaded the suitcase and backpack into the trunk of her car. "I'll drop you off and then go pack a bag."

Of course, Morgan knew just what she needed. A night with her sister but a few moments to herself.

Spencer agreed and watched as her little sister skipped back around to the driver's side. After inhaling a deep breath, she glanced back at the automatic doors. They closed, open. How easily she could have returned inside, booked another ticket, and hopped on the next flight. She thought about extending her trip more than a few times, but she had unfinished business back home. And Hawai'i was home. Hawai'i would always be home.

She opened the door for herself, tucked herself inside, and turned on the radio. Mr. Brightside filled the air. Spencer smiled.

As soon as Spencer made it home, she dropped her belongings by the front door and made her way to her bedroom. It didn't hit her until after the fact that she didn't bother checking to see if he had taken all of his things. She was a girl on a mission. And he was so yesterday's news.

Her closet was a mess, as always. But she knew exactly what she was looking for and where it waited for her.

Spencer dug through all the clothes, the junk, the old and forgotten memories. In the back corner, she kept a small box that held various birthday cards and letters received over the years, mostly from her childhood. Right at the top sat the envelope received five years ago from San Francisco—untouched, unblemished. It looked as it did the day it arrived.

She paused for a second, took a deep breath, and then finally read it.